RULES WE BREAK

J. WILDER

To everyone who encouraged me to write this short smutty novella.

AUTHOR'S NOTE

IN CASE YOU MISSED IT, Rules We Break is a companion novella to Rules Of Our Own. I highly suggest reading it first if you want any relationship development. They're fully together in this book.

This book is mostly smut. If you're looking for a plot driven story, you will not find it here.

5 out of 8 chapters are spicy.

Have fun!

Join Jessa's readers' FB group. **ARC SIGN UP EXCLUSIVE**. I love to share sneak peeks while writing and you'll be the first to see anything new. I'm dying to hear what you think!

CHAPTER 1
ALEX

I READY myself for the faceoff, my stick pressing against the hard surface of the ice. The score is tied three-three and the Detroit crowd is going crazy. I scan the stands already knowing I won't see the pale blonde hair and crisp green eyes I'm searching for. Mia's shifts have doubled since starting at the hospital while maintaining her time at the clinic just over a month ago. Some nights she gets home and she's so tired that it takes everything in me not to collect her in my arms and drag her back to bed. But that's not what she needs from us.

River and I aren't holding her back or hiding her away. Fuck that. Mia's the most determined person I know and that's saying something considering I'm surrounded by professional athletes. It would be a fucking travesty if anyone tried to discourage her. So, yeah. She can't come to our away games, but it just makes getting home to her all the more sweet.

As if he called my name, my eyes snap to meet

River's. His piercing dark gaze heats my chest, and suddenly the score doesn't matter because all I want is to get him off the ice and back where I can have him alone. The way his tongue travels over his bottom lip has me so distracted I nearly miss the fucking whistle. My stick is barely fast enough to catch the puck off the faceoff.

Booing rings out through the arena as I fake around the opposing defenseman. I break past the second D-man and head straight for the net. The crisp air cools my cheeks as I make eye contact with the goalie, not looking away even as I line up my shot. I shift to the left, exaggerating my movements, letting my weight tip over my knee so the goalie buys into my fake and quickly rebound to the right.

The moment before I fire off my shot, a solid wall slams into me sending a shockwave through my back and propelling me off my feet. It's a dirty fucking hit, and I'm too close to the net to avoid the inevitable collision. The steel red bar hits the side of my helmet with a loud crack milliseconds before my shoulder takes the full brunt of my weight and I drop to my knees.

"Fuck." I groan through my teeth, clenching my jaw at the shattering pain I can barely breathe through. The impact steals my senses momentarily and I stay there frozen, head ringing as the world slowly comes back into focus. Someone is yelling behind me, and it takes a second to make out River's voice.

I turn, dropping my ass to the ice and my dick

twitches at the sight before me. River's towering over the player who'd laid me out. Their helmets and gloves are off, already deep into the fight and blood trickles down the other guy's mouth. The fact that his eye is already swelling, tells me he's in for a hell of a black eye.

I lean back on my elbows both because the world spins around me and cause I'm enjoying the show. River cussing him out, in a low growl that I can only make out because we're so close. "I will fucking kill you."

If I was that guy, I'd be scared for my fucking life with the way Riv's tearing into him.

With a beauty of a move, River reaches around and yanks the guy's jersey so hard it breaks the strap attaching it to his pants. It's ripped off then pulled over his head. It's been a long fucking time since I've seen someone get jerseyed.

"Alright, break it up." Lucas cuts between them, and pushes them apart. River gives him a sharp look, and Lucas just stares right back. "Go look after your boy, I've got the asshole."

River's head snaps to mine and he doesn't waste time crouching down to look into my eyes. He unclips my helmet, and removes it, careful not to jostle me. His eyes search my face, his expression pained, and his brows pinched with worry.

"He's fucking dead."

Fuck me, warmth builds in my stomach and my already hard cock aches for him. There's nothing sexier than a protective River when he's all riled up like this. The way he's looking at me like he might take me right here on the rink just to prove I'm okay, has me groaning through my teeth. Ever since he admitted he loved me, he's been nothing but fucking trouble.

"Pull me up." I reach out my hand and River's fingers curve around mine easily lifting my over two-hundred-pound weight until I'm standing on my skates.

He puts his hands on my shoulders, steadying me when my knees threaten to give out.

"Your shoulder okay?" he asks softly.

I shrug. "I've had worse."

He grips the back of my neck and pulls me so our foreheads rest against each other. "I swear to God, the crack that crash made took years off my life." He's still breathing hard from either the fight, adrenaline, or what I hope is the proximity to me.

I bury my fingers in his coal black hair and pull him imperceptibly closer. Just far enough to still be decent. "I'm okay. I promise."

River's shoulders collapse with his sigh of release. "Thank God."

His hold on me doesn't loosen as we skate to the bench, even after I reassure him I'm fine. If anything, his grip tightens, like even the idea of me being away from him right now is more than he can take.

The team doctor gestures me into the back, forcing River to let go.

"I'll see you back there—" River starts, but Lucas cuts in.

"As soon as we're done kicking their ass."

I hate the idea of leaving the game with only a few minutes left, but I can practically hear Mia explaining all the different worries that come with concussions. I once made the mistake of telling her they're a part of the sport, then had to go through a several hour training session on why I was wrong. Not that I minded, since she sat in my lap the entire time. She could be talking about knitting and I'd still be riveted by her every single word.

Doc sits me on the locker bench and runs through the regular concussion protocol. "Any nausea?"

"None." I say trying not to blink against the bright light.

"List four players on your team."

"Davis, King, Leduc, Thompson." I rattle them off and do my best not to roll my eyes.

I must do a shit job of it because he lifts a pale brow in disappointment. "Alright, I think you're good. Do me a favor and don't hit it again for a few games."

"Sure thing coach." I mean I always try not to hit my head. It's not like it's intentional.

He makes an unimpressed sound and checks out my shoulder. "You'll be bruised, but nothing's broken."

"Already knew that." I wasn't kidding when I told River I've had worse. An injury like this is standard enough that, after the initial shock wore off, I knew I'd be fine.

The doc stands, packs up his stuff, then leaves me

alone in the locker room. The walls are covered by green painted lockers, and polished wood benches. All things considered, it's one of the better changing rooms I've been in. There's a large screen on the far wall, playing the game. I watch as Lucas passes the puck from the D-zone up to where River's waiting for it right before the blue line. Detroit didn't stand a chance, and they're stuck trying to catch up as River tears down the rink heading to the undefended goalie.

I can practically see River's smile from here as the puck slides between the goalie's pads. His once scarce smiles have become his regular go to. I'm sure I can speak for Mia when I say he knows how to use them. He's had us both tied up, literally and figuratively, begging for more with a simple hint of a grin. Not that I'm complaining.

The crowd's silent as they shuffle out, but my guys are cheering as they make their way down the tunnel to the locker room. Lucas is first through the door, smiling wide. "Fuck yes, buddy!"

I nod at him. It was a solid assist, but I'm not inflating his ego anymore. Piper does that enough for the both of us.

"Move." River's low timber cuts through the room, and Lucas practically jumps out of the way. His normally smart-ass quips caught on his tongue.

River rips off his helmet and doesn't stop until he's directly in front of me. "You clear?"

"Yeah, all good."

"Good." He leans down and crashes his lips to

RULES WE BREAK   9

mine. The room goes blank as I open for him, the soft edge of his tongue rolling over mine. I moan, lifting forward to take more of the kiss, searching for everything he can give me, not giving a single shit who sees.

"Get a fucking room." Someone yells from the lockers across the room. Unsurprisingly, the guys took the news that we're dating well, but that doesn't stop them from giving us shit whenever they can.

River breaks the kiss, and nips my bottom lip before pulling away. "I plan on it."

Coach claps, drawing our attention. "Alright, alright. Settle down. You all played an excellent game tonight. As you know, we've spent entirely too long without a captain and tonight I think he proved himself."

My stomach clenches and my gut twists. I'd wanted the captaincy since college, but back then it went to Lucas instead. I kept my shit together then, but I'm so close now. I can't help but glance over at River. He's already smiling at me, and it's not until Lucas shakes my shoulder that I register the guys cheering.

"Congrats, Cap. You're going to do great."

If it wouldn't kill him, I swear coach would be rolling his eyes right now. I never once said I didn't get distracted.

"Speech!" The guys start yelling, and I stand.

"Okay, okay, settle down. You've all played well this year, but I'm going to expect the best from each of you. Now, suck it up for next practice." I give them a playful smile. "Hell, we all know I was destined for this."

My words are met with jeering and followed by more congratulations. We spend an extra twenty minutes longer than usual before we get into the showers.

I tip my head back letting the warm spray wash over my hair, and cascade over my sore shoulder. The showers here are pretty standard. White tiled walls separating each stall, bench for my stuff, and a floor length curtain blocking off the entry. Prior to joining the NHL I thought everything would be top of the line luxury. Turns out I was one hundred percent wrong on that.

Eyes closed, I rotate my arm, and do my best to ignore the tightness as I loosen the joint. I push through the pain, knowing the worst thing I can do now is let it stiffen.

I barely register the sound of someone behind me before fingers close around my mouth. "Quiet."

I jerk only to be pulled against a very solid, very naked chest. I shudder as River murmurs into my ear. "Let me see."

I check the curtain quickly, but it's drawn closed. He's quiet for such a big bastard. River runs his free hand over my shoulder, grazing the sensitive skin until my skin pebbles under his touch. His other hand stays planted firmly over my mouth, catching every sound I make. A shudder runs down my spine, starting where his lips graze my neck and his teeth clamp around the soft lobe of my ear. "Don't do that again."

He and I both know it's a part of the game, but my laugh is cut off by the tender press of his lips against the sorest area of my shoulder. He slowly caresses every single inch of my rapidly bruising skin, careful not to press too hard. I lean my weight against him and drop my head to the side to give him better access. He eagerly licks a path along the skin, swiping up the pooling water in the hollow above my collar bone. He closes the remaining space between us and his cock presses against my ass. I clench my teeth, but nearly lose it when he slides his palm down my chest, along my abs, and grasps the base of my cock in his hard grip.

He doesn't stroke me, instead he squeezes and lets go, pulsing until my eyes are rolling back and my hips are fighting against his grasp to force him to pump me like I need.

He chuckles against my ear, his low voice coming out in command. "I said, don't do that again. Are you going to listen, Baby?"

Suddenly there's nothing funny about that question and I'm nodding my head, the back of my head still pressed against his shoulder.

"Good boy." He strokes my cock from base to tip, then uses his thumb to coat the head before stroking down, only to do it again. I'm a panting fucking mess as I thrust into his grip, chasing my release. Fucking grateful for his hand muffling the indecent noises threatening to escape.

"You like that, Baby? You like it when I wrap you in my fist?" He punctuates his words with a hard twist.

I moan and my eyes roll back, not able to do anything but let him control me. His cock thrusts against my ass matching the rhythm of his hand, and I suddenly need him inside me anyway I can. I twist my face to the left, breaking free of his fingers covering my mouth. Ignoring his low growl, I drop to my knees in front of him. His abdomen flexes, deep cut muscles angled down toward his cock bobbing in the space between us. The swollen tip begging for my mouth. I move forward, sucking on it, before driving him deep into my throat.

His salty taste fills my mouth and it's his turn to lose control. I pull off of him, and watch him with hooded eyes only long enough for him to stumble against the wall. I swallow him down again, swirling my tongue, basking in the way he jerks deeper, like he can't fucking help it. I grasp his balls, rolling them in my palm, and he groans entirely too loud for our current location.

I pull back. "You need to be quiet or they'll hear you."

He smirks. "Who said I don't want them to hear me?"

My smile is cut off when his fingers dig into my hair, hard enough to hurt and he thrusts deep into my mouth. I gag around him, and take quick breaths every time he pulls back because there's nothing more that I want than for him to fuck my face like he can't stop himself.

I grasp his hips, yank him harder and swallow around him like I know he likes. His grip tightens and his breathing grows rapid with his approaching release. My mouth fills with saliva, ready to taste him on my tongue.

He jerks my head back. "Fuck, Baby."

I stare up at him from my knees, his hand still fisted in my hair waiting for him to tell me what he wants next. He doesn't make me wait long.

"Get up, hands on the wall."

I stand, facing the wall, and plant my hands like I'm being fucking arrested. I watch River grab a small silver packet of lube from where he's placed his towel on the bench.

"Next time I'll take my time getting you ready. I want you too bad to stop."

I nod eagerly, because at this point, my dick's aching so bad I'd let him tear me apart if it meant getting him inside me.

My body shakes as he rounds behind me, and his fingers circle my hole until I'm rocking back against him.

"Fuck, Riv stop edging me."

He leans forward and smiles against my neck. "Never."

I like the way that sounds an awful lot like forever.

He slides two lubed fingers into my ass, before

pulling them out to circle the rim and thrust them back in. I stretch around him, breathing through it.

"Relax, baby. I've got you." He murmurs into my neck.

It's the softness of his tone that has me collapsing forward against my forearms and my body turning to putty in his hands. Whatever he asks of me, it's his.

He pulls his fingers out and I can't stop the moan from escaping my lips when it's immediately replaced by the thick blunt tip of his cock.

Someone clears their throat on the other side of the curtain, and I freeze. Shit.

"Hurry the fuck up. You're the last one out." It's the fucking rookie and if he knows we're in here, so does everyone else.

My cheeks start to heat, a blush climbing up my neck. I go to shift away, expecting River to pull back, but his chest presses against my back and he buries his cock inside me in one swift move.

Holy fucking shit.

I can barely suck in a breath before he does it again.

"You feel that? So fucking good, stretched wide around me." He thrust again. "You take me so well, Baby."

Fuck me. I press back against him, trying to speed him up. He chuckles against my shoulder and reaches around my waist to grasp my cock again.

This time it's more than I can take and I start to thrust back and forth searching for my release.

River runs his teeth along the shell of my ear. "Beg for it."

"Fucking Christ." I groan. "Please. River, please fuck me."

His control snaps and he bites into my shoulder, his cock slamming into my ass over and over as his fist strokes my cock. I don't bother trying to be quiet. The entire team could come in and nothing could stop what's happening right now.

His fingers clench almost painfully and my release crashes through me, my body shuddering with every spurt of my release.

"That's it, Baby." River's strokes slow, and grow languid as I come down from my orgasm. Once I've steadied myself, he grips the back of my neck, pressing my face hard into the wall. The cool tile digging into my cheek while he fucks me with abandon. The sharp snap of his thrust echo through the room as he chases his own release over the edge with a deep rumbling moan. "Alex."

Breathing heavily, he kisses the nape of my neck tenderly. "You're going to kill me."

"The feeling's fucking mutual." I grind out, fully collapsed against the wall, not even shifting as he pulls out. I'm like jelly, clinging onto the cool white tile for balance. River washes me and the sweet smell of his body wash fills the air. He has a thing about marking us with his smell and the deepest, primal part of me isn't mad about it.

He flips me around, washing my front and drops

his head to mine. Dark eyes search my face. "I love you."

No matter how many times he says it, my stomach still flips. "I love you too."

He bites my lower lip before pulling back. "Let's get home to our girl."

CHAPTER 2
RIVER

I WATCH Alex get ready across the room as I meticulously roll the sleeves of my crisp button up shirt, revealing my forearms. By the time we'd made it out of the shower, the rest of the guys were already out in the hall. Alex had turned a cute shade of pink, but all I felt was a possessive sense of pride.

I swear to fucking God, Alex is taking his sweet time pulling on his shirt. He's facing his locker, joggers hung low on his hips, and the muscles of his back ripple with his movements. I have half a mind to drag him back into the shower. The bright white fabric slips down his spine and I let out a breath.

If this man knew how gone I am for him…no screw that, I want him to know. I want him to fucking scream it from the rooftops. I close the distance between us with three long strides, wrap my arms around his middle and bury my face into his neck, taking a deep breath.

He leans into me and says, "I'm never going to finish getting ready if you touch me like this."

I splay my palm over his stomach and bite my bottom lip as his muscles flex underneath. "That's not the deterrent you think it is."

He chuckles and spins in my arms. His eyes widen when I press closer, crowding him until his back hits the locker.

"Anything you want. Ask and it's yours." I say, fingers tightening on my hip.

His head tilts to the side as he takes me in, and with one brow arched Alex asks. "Anything?"

I nod, not knowing what I can give him that he doesn't have, but wanting to do it anyway.

"Bugatti Chiron." He blurts out, smiling like he doesn't believe me.

"Done."

He tilts his head. "Serious?"

"Dead fucking serious."

"Fuck off." He scoffs.

I lean in and nip his bottom lip, promising. "Later."

He gulps and clears his throat. "Well, what do you want?"

"You and Mia. Fuck everything and everyone else."

"Hey, no fair that you say something like that after I asked for a car."

I shrug, a smirk pulling at the corner of my mouth. "No one said anything about being fair."

I step away and he grips my arm, tugging me to

face him. His face is all sharp, serious angles. "You know it's like that for me too, right? The car, the money, hell, the fucking game. You both come first. *Always*."

He's cute when he's all charming. I grip his jaw and capture his mouth with mine, eating his moans. I don't stop until he turns pliant in my arms. I grab his hoodie from the bench, noting it's the one Mia likes to wear around the apartment with nothing underneath. Handing it to him I say. "Come on, before they send Coach in to get us."

I pull open the heavy wood door and spot Lucas leaning against the wall across from us smirking like a Cheshire cat. "Well, well. What were you two doing?"

I cross my arms casually and lean against the door frame to match his positioning. "Exactly what you think we were doing."

Alex makes a half cough, half choking sound. "How the fuck am I the shy one now?"

Lucas kicks off the wall and guides us out the door. "I don't know but it's fucking hilarious. Everyone's already out there. I drew the short straw coming back to get you."

"Short straw?" Alex asks.

"Yeah, no one wanted to deal with a pissed off River when we interrupted you two getting off."

Alex turns bright red, and bites the side of his cheek. I swipe my thumb over the indent it leaves until he lets it go. "Don't worry. I wouldn't stop just because they walked in."

Goosebumps erupt down his neck, and if I don't stop this soon, we're going to miss our flight.

I step back and shove my hands into my pockets to prevent myself from reaching out again. Lucas notes the action with another smirk.

I'd roll my eyes if I didn't think Lucas would think it was fucking hilarious.

"Come on. Piper's waiting for me back home and if I'm late because of you two she's going to have words."

The idea of Piper yelling at us, is surprisingly motivating. She's not very big, but growing up around Lucas, Jax and her brother gave her an edge in an argument.

"We're already ready, relax." Alex says, and heads down the hall, opening the door to where our bus waits for us. Snowflakes drift all around us, melting the second they hit the ground.

We fly between games, but the bus is the most efficient way to get us, and all our gear to and from the airport.

I follow Alex onto the bus, and the second he turns into the aisle the space fills with the team's jeering. Every possible lew thing that can be said is said. I grab Alex's pack from his shoulder and throw it up in the overhead bin.

"I'd say don't be jealous, but you absolutely should be." I say loud enough for the entire bus to hear.

Alex takes the window seat and I sit down beside him. The coach bus is specially made for us. They've taken out several seats to make more room. I stretch my legs out in front of me, and settle in when I feel Alex's gaze hot on the side of my face.

I turn to him, raising a brow. "What?"

"Just wondering when you got so talkative?"

His teeth sink into his bottom lip, and I lift my hand to palm his face, running my thumb across his lip, and pulling it free. Goosebumps erupt down his neck and he visibly shivers. I meet his warm brown eyes. "When I started thinking of you as mine."

"Oh." It comes out on a little gasp.

"Yeah, oh." I lean in and kiss his forehead. No matter how much I want to push this further, even I'm not comfortable fucking him on the team bus. Plus, I need him ready to go again when we get home to Mia. I've been craving her like a drowning man's last breath.

Alex rests his head on my shoulder, adjusting himself so he's angled into me, and flips through his phone. It's lit up with notifications, and I lean in over his shoulder to read them.

Jax: Congratulations, Buddy. Knew they'd have to give it to you eventually.

Sidney: What Jax means is you deserve it.

Jax: Is that what I mean?

Sidney: …

Jax: Alright. Yes, Sid's right. You deserve it.

Alex chuckles at that and it vibrates against my chest.

Piper: Congratulations! We should do something to celebrate.

Mia: Yes! Maybe when Sidney and Jax come for Christmas next week?

The next few messages are just the three girls making plans. Dinner on the Friday and then Christmas present opening on the Saturday morning.

Mia texts Alex and I in our private chat.

Mia: Congrats, Alex. Can't wait for you to come home so we can celebrate.

He shifts in his seat, and I drop my arm around his shoulder.

Alex: Soon, Kitten.

Mia: How soon?

I take out my phone, sending her a quick message.

Me: Still an hour before we're home. Get ready for us, okay?

Mia: Not going to be a problem.

The idea of Mia at our apartment. Sitting, waiting for us, has my head spinning.

I shove my phone back into my pocket, settling myself into my seat, when Alex stiffens beside me. This time he's moved his phone lower, out of my line of sight, so I covertly crane around his shoulder. Is it a complete violation of his privacy? Yes. Do I give a single shit when he's frozen beside me. Not for a single second.

Alex: Hey, mom.

Alex: They made me captain.

Mom: Does it come with a raise?

Alex pauses for several seconds before replying.

Alex: No.

Mom: Too bad, Dear. Did you hear your brother's been nominated for the Jonesville award. It's not until January, will you be able to make it?

Alex: Sure. Sounds like my friends are going to put together a celebration dinner. I would love to see you there.

Mom: I'll check our schedule. Your brother has a lot of activities this winter.

Alex's shoulders droop, and he takes a deep breath, holding it for several seconds before releasing it. Rage builds in my gut. I want to rip the phone from his hands and lay into her for every time she makes him feel less than. Alex's brother is two years younger than him, but since he chose athletics and not academia, they've basically treated him like a burden.

Alex must sense it because he closes his phone, and shoves it in my bag. One of these days I'm going to tell her every single thing I think of her. Starting with her being a piece of shit mom for never looking at Alex with any source of pride, when there are so many things about him to be proud of.

Not today. Tonight's all about celebrating him. I run my nose along the shell of his ear, sending a shiver through him. "I'm proud of you."

He turns his head and kisses me in response.

———

The plane lands hard, jerking us in our seats. Alex

fell asleep a half hour ago, and he sits up straight looking at me with sleepy eyes and a surge of love fills me. Fuck his parents. I'm going to show him exactly how deliciously special he is.

After years of repeating the same thing. Alex and I are efficient at grabbing our shit and getting into his car. Within ten minutes we're on the road, making it the fifteen-minute drive to our apartment.

River: Landed, see you soon.

Mia doesn't text back right away, and a muscle ticks in my cheeks waiting for her reply. Even though Jason was hauled back to Canada, I still didn't like leaving her alone.

My phone buzzes and I nearly drop it as a video of Mia stretched out on the bed, completely naked fills my screen. I connect the sound to the car speaker and it's immediately filled with Mia's moans, and the indecent sound her fingers make as she sinks them into her soaking pussy.

Alex nearly swerves off the road, and I have to grab the wheel to keep us steady.

His fingers white knuckle on the steering wheel. "What the fuck is that?"

"Our girl, getting ready for us."

"Fuck me." He hisses through clenched teeth, and I can already make out the ridge of his rapidly hardening cock.

I lean forward, and growl into his ear. "I plan on it."

I'm forced back into my seat by the sheer force of

his acceleration. He's cutting the time down from fifteen to ten.

River: Don't finish without us.

Mia: Not fair.

River: The only place you're coming is on my tongue.

Dots come and go on the bottom of the screen until her message appears.

Mia: Hurry.

River: Soon, Love. Soon you'll be under us, screaming our fucking names while we take turns on that sweet pussy of yours.

She doesn't respond, and the picture of her, fingers clenched into the blanket, holding herself together as she tries to obey my command, has me painfully hard.

The car jumps over the curb, pulling into the valet section of our apartment. It's a testament to just how eager Alex is to get to our girl that he'd risk damaging it. We're out of the car in seconds, striding through the front door.

Alex tosses his keys to the attendant without stopping. "Take care of this for me please. There's a big tip in it for you."

The valet's eyes light up and he nods rapidly. We never come around back, Alex hating the idea of anyone else driving his car. But tonight, neither of us are willing to waste the precious seconds parking it ourselves.

We're through the lobby and into the elevator, impatiently listening to the chime when we pass each floor. For the first time ever, I loathe that we have the upper floor apartment. Alex shifts on his feet beside me, and I pin him to the wall, knocking the air out of him. My cock is rigid against his, and the only thing stopping me from hitting the emergency stop button, pulling his cock out, and taking it in my mouth is the knowledge that Mia's waiting for us, her cum dripping down her thighs.

The elevator jerks when we stop, and I grasp Alex's wrist dragging him out. Not that it's necessary. He's matching me stride for stride. He twists the doorknob, and I'm happy to see she locked it. He fumbles with his keys, and I take them from him, fingers gliding against his and my cock twitches at the contact. We're so fucking close.

I head straight to our room, and groan at the sight of her. The video she sent is nothing compared to the real thing. Her blonde hair fans around her face, her chest is arched off the bed, and her fingers are dug into the mattress. She's fidgeting, her mouth dropped open, and a low adorable growl escapes her lips.

"River, I need you now. I'm so close. It hurts."

Fuck. My mouth is on her pussy instantly, and I moan as her sweet taste coats my tongue. She arches off the bed and I pin her hips down so she can't reach for the friction she desperately desires. I lick her wetness off the inside of her thighs, teasing her until she's begging me, like the good fucking girl she is. Her fingers are dangerously close to ripping out my hair and I chuckle, my mouth pressed firmly into her center.

I avoid her tight bundle of nerves and fuck her with my tongue. Her moans turn impossibly more desperate as she chases the release I'm not ready to give her. I need her crying for us before I'll give her what she wants.

She's not the only one suffering. My cock's buried into the mattress, not nearly enough pressure to reach my own orgasm. But between the taste of her and her needy sounds, I'm about to lose my own mind.

Alex's firm fingers grip my hips, make quick work of my belt. He forces me to lift so he can pull my pants off my hips, leaving me exposed to him. He palms my ass, spreading it apart, and I growl into Mia's pussy, devouring her.

Alex's warm mouth covers my asshole and I fucking lose myself to the intense sensation. My dick's leaking all over the fucking place and I grip Mia's thighs, guiding them back, so her knees are bent beside my head and I can get a deeper angle. I rock back, my balls tightening as pressure builds low in my gut. I need Mia to fucking cum, because I'm about to cover her in mine.

I suck her clit hard, basking in her screaming our names, before lightly biting it. A shudder rocks through her, shaking her entire body, as she comes on my mouth. Her orgasm triggers my own and I lift onto my knees, spurting my cum all over her breasts. She looks up at me, mouth open with her pants, and she looks fucking perfect painted with my release.

Alex comes up beside me, and gently pushes me

so I collapse on the bed beside her. He's completely naked, and his pre-cum is dripping from his tip. My mouth waters. I want to lick it off and feel the weight of his cock on my tongue but before I can move, he leans down and licks a path through my cum, twirling his tongue in her navel cleaning every ounce of me off her.

Alex grips her jaw, opening it for him, her wide eyes searching. He leans in and lets my thick liquid drip into her mouth.

Holy shit.

She moans, swallowing every drop.

Closing the distance between them, he licks where it smeared her chin, before taking her mouth in a desperate kiss.

Fuck. I'm normally the one in control, but there's an edge to him. Like he fucking needs this and I'm happy to give it to him.

Alex grips Mia's hips and flips her onto her stomach, climbing over her back and growling into her hair. "You have no idea how badly I want to fuck this sweet ass of yours. You want that, Kitten?"

She presses against him, and her voice comes out as a raspy plea. "Yes."

He groans into her neck while I grab the lube from the nightstand and slap his hand away when he tries to take it. Instead, I slide my hand between them, forcing him to raise up so I can wrap his cock in my fist, the lube allowing him to glide easily through my firm grip. He groans low, and his muscles shift as a shudder rolls through him.

Mia meets my gaze, the green of her eyes taken over by her blown wide pupils. Alex hasn't done this before and it's a thrill for Mia and I to be his first. I guide him to her back hole, never looking away from her. She nods. "Now, Alex."

That's all it takes for him to press the head of his cock into her ass, and fill her one inch at a time. I watch where they connect, each of his pumps turning more uncontrolled than the next. "Fuck, Baby. You're so perfect, buried in our girl."

Alex lifts onto his knees, taking her with him and starts to pound his cock into her. Her moans grow louder as she approaches her second release, and it just pushes him harder. The two of them look so fucking good, lost in their own desire, that they don't notice me stripping out of my shirt until my lubed cock is pressed against Alex's ass.

He chokes on a breath, slamming to the hilt, and Mia looks back with a devious smile.

"I'm going to fuck him into you, Love."

Her eyes roll back, and her fingers dig into the mattress getting ready for us.

I kiss the nape of Alex's neck, rubbing the head of my cock against his tight hole. I'm on my knees behind him. His back to my front, giving me the perfect angle. I push further, just barely breaching him.

"You want this, Baby?"

"Fuck, yes." He rocks back, not pulling all the way out of Mia and I slam into him, driving him forward until he's buried deep. The dual sensation has him wild between us and I fuck him into her harder, and harder. My cock slipping in and out of his tight hole. He whimpers when I slam back into him.

"Fuck me. Fuck me. Fuck me." Tumbles from his mouth on repeat as I do just that. "I'm so fucking close."

I pause deep inside him, and he whines at the back of his throat.

"Take care of our girl." I command and his hand reaches under her to play with her clit. She collapses to her forearms, desperate cries escaping her mouth as her orgasm takes her over in shuddering waves.

I fuck them both, milking every last drop of her release, before wrapping my palm around Alex's throat from behind, like I know he likes, and take over. I fuck him mercilessly until he's shaking so hard, it vibrates through me. He yells out his release while I fill his ass with my own. It takes several breaths before I'm steady enough to pull out of him, then collapse to the side of the bed, pulling him with me.

We shift so Mia's between us, her face buried in my chest and Alex wrapped around her from behind. They're both asleep within seconds. I can't though. I'm obsessed with the way they look together. With the fact that I know they're one-hundred percent mine. I may not deserve them, but I'll never let them go.

CHAPTER 3
MIA

SUN STREAMS through the bedroom window and I slowly ascend into consciousness. My nose is buried in a hard chest and I breath in River's masculine scent until my head clears. The covers pull tight as a weight shifts behind me, followed by a loud thump.

"We need a bigger bed." Alex groans from where he landed on the floor.

I giggle and River's hand travels up my back to gently cup my neck. "Now that you're both living with me, do you think we need some new furniture?"

Warmth floods me at his words. I love knowing they both want me here, and the fact that they're willing to make changes to accommodate us has flutters forming in my chest. "As much as I love to cuddle you both, I think another foot or two of room is needed."

Alex crawls back into the bed and drags my back

to his chest. "I'll give you a foot." It's playful more than anything, and I roll my eyes.

"A foot, eh?"

His fingers travel up my sides, until they brush the sensitive spot just below my ribs and I wiggle to try to get out of his grasp. "What are you trying to say? You don't think between the two of us you get more than a foot?"

Heat floods my core, picture just how full they make me, and I rub my thighs together at his low, growly tone. We need to get out of this bed before we never get up. I break free of Alex's grasp and go to climb over him. He's so big I have to lift one leg over him at a time and he stops me, both hands on my hips while I'm straddling him.

My nipples are peaked, visible through my t-shirt, and his gaze narrows in on them. At some point last night, River had woken us up to shower and I threw on one of Alex's shirts before crawling back into bed. His cock is nestled against my bare pussy, the tip pressed against my core and I know we're not getting out of here any time soon.

A low meow comes through the crack under the door. We started locking Crookshanks out after an incident where he became a little too curious about Alex's naked body.

"He's probably hungry." I lift, and Alex helps me off the bed mumbling something about ungrateful cats.

He looks so put out, I laugh and kiss him. My lips barely graze his before Crookshanks meows again.

Alex's eyes narrow on the door, but I know he's all bluff. Both River and Alex treat Crookshanks like he's part of the family.

River's the first to get dressed, pulling on a pair of workout shorts and not bothering with a shirt, leaving his sharp cut muscles on full display. I swallow hard, contemplating just opening the cat food bag and dragging them both back to bed, before River says,

"I'll put on coffee. Breakfast then shopping."

My stomach growls loudly at that, and both guys grin at me. We move around each other in the kitchen in a now familiar dance. As if we'd been doing this for years instead of months. I watch Alex run his hand down River's ass, giving it a squeeze before flipping a pancake in the pan.

River turns to me brow lifted. "If you keep looking at us like that, we'll never go shopping."

I hum. "I like the sound of that."

Alex slides a plate stacked with pancakes in front of me before smothering it with syrup. "Eat, you'll need your energy for later."

"Later?" I press my thighs together, and do my best not to squirm in my seat.

"Later." His reply comes out as a promise.

I collapse back onto the mattress. We've been at the store for over an hour, feeling out each one. I swear River's worse than Goldie Locks looking for the perfect firmness. He collapses beside me, and a low hum vibrates from his chest. Good sign.

"So, you like the hard ones?" The red-headed saleswomen says, a little too close to a completely oblivious Alex. For someone who'd considered himself a player, he's definitely missed all the signs since we've been together.

"I guess. I mean they're all pretty much the same." He responds looking through the rows of mattress, no doubt searching for us.

She leans in, her hand wrapping around his forearm as she says something too low for us to hear. Alex's brows pull together, and he pulls away from her.

River growls menacingly behind me and I can't help my smile. There's something about his jealousy that I freaking love. Not that he has anything to worry about, which if I think about it, just makes it that much hotter.

River's up and strolling toward them. His black button up sleeves rolled to his elbows and his shined dress shoes click on the floor. He immediately pulls a surprised Alex's back against his chest and bands his arm around his stomach possessively.

"We found one." River dips his head into the crook of Alex's neck and speaks loud enough for all of us to hear him. "Go lay with our girl and see how it feels with her."

The saleswoman steps back in shock, eyes wide as she mouths the words "Our girl."

Yeah lady. What did you think we were when we came in here?

Alex makes his way over to me, and the bed sinks where he lays beside me, pulling me into his arms and running his teeth along the soft lobe of my ear. "Do you think he knows how fucking sexy he is when he gets all jealous?"

"I hope he never stops." My chuckle escapes me first, followed by his.

He stretches out on the bed, and a frown pulls down his mouth. "I don't like being this far from you."

A laugh burst from me. "You're literally inches from me."

River comes in behind me. "He's right. We stick with the king."

"But you're freaking huge and we're practically laying over each other." I complain, but there's no real heart behind it. I love waking up tangled between them.

"That's the point, Love. We don't want any room."

The saleswoman comes toward us, seemingly recovered from her shock. "Is this the winner?"

River sits up, pulling me with him, then holds up his hand to guide me to stand. He entwines our fingers. "We're not interested."

There's an edge to his voice that hints at something more and Alex's soft chuckle tells me he heard it too.

When we're out of the store and in Alex's car, I'm squished in the back seat. The sports model isn't truly designed for three people and a quick glance back from Alex has him saying, "I'll pick up a different one tomorrow."

"A different car?"

"Yeah, something big enough for the three of us."

My breath hitches, I love it when they're sweet like this. "You don't have to."

He arches a brow then puts the car in drive. "I want to. Now, let's get you home so we can set up the tree."

A thrill goes through me at the idea of our first Christmas together.

———

Christmas music floods through the hidden speakers in our apartment. It's still taking me time to adjust to just how rich they really are. I have a few more years working at the hospital before they'll pay me a decent wage but, against what I previously believed, I'm more than happy to let the two of them spend their money on me. Hell, I'm pretty sure it would hurt River if he couldn't take care of us.

The door opens, revealing a disheveled River and Alex, dragging a cart with a massive Christmas tree on it. The smell of pine instantly filling the air and bringing a smile to my lips.

They push the cart inside and that's when I spot the boxes of decorations. I hop on the balls of my feet, practically vibrating with giddiness, and I immediately start digging through the boxes.

River and Alex lift the tree easily, moving it to the stand I already set up, not even attempting to move me out of the way.

The box is filled with multicolored ornaments, in all shapes and sizes. Everything I could possibly want and love. Nothing like I'd expect River to have. "Where are these from?"

River blushes a pretty shade of pink and my heart skips. "I ordered them online." He looks nervous and so unlike his normal self.

"Love them." I say, already nose deep in the boxes again when they have the tree set up. I turn back with a string of Christmas lights in my hand that River's eyes focus on. Tingles travel down my spine at the way he's looking at me.

I swallow hard as images of being wrapped up in these lights flash in my brain and River's smirk tells me he knows exactly what I'm thinking.

Alex's phone rings before anything can come of it.

He answers. "Hey, Mom."

I can't make out what she's saying but whatever it is has Alex's shoulder folding in, and he nods his head dejectedly even though his mom can't see him.

"No, no, it's okay. I understand."

Whatever she's saying on the other line it's definitely not okay. A pit of unease forms in my stomach and worry takes over me. By the time Alex hangs up the phone, everything about him screams disappointment.

I stride up to him and wrap my arms around his middle. It's a testament of how he's feeling that he doesn't give me his usual beaming smile. Instead, his lips tip up in the corner in a mockery of his usual grin.

I grab his cheeks in my hands and pull his forehead to mine. "What happened?"

"Nothing."

"Do not nothing me. We're a team. What happened?"

He shrugs. "My parents can't make it to the dinner. Like I said. It's nothing."

"Why? Why can't they make it?" It's no secret that Alex's family have never celebrated his accomplishments and my skin's heating with the force of my anger.

"My brother has some kind of thing that day."

"What kind of thing? Like an award?"

"No. No, like a zoom call or something with some boss. She didn't really get into it."

Rage flashes through me. "Are. You. Kidding. Me? They canceled over your brother's freaking Zoom call? That's why they can't come?"

"It's okay, Kitten." Alex gives me a sad smile. "I didn't expect them to come anyway."

I growl low in my throat. "Whatever this is, it's absolutely not okay." I turn to River who looks just as pissed as I feel. "Do you still have that friend with the private jet?"

A dark smile curves his lips. "You going to confront them, Love?"

"No one hurts what's mine."

CHAPTER 4
MIA

BY THE TIME I'm standing in front of Alex's childhood home, I'm practically vibrating with pent up emotions. Anger, disgust, sadness all tumble in my stomach. The Graysons are about to get a big surprise.

Alex had mentioned to them that I was in town and stopping by to collect some ancient trophy he'd left at their place. His mom basically said they're hidden somewhere in the basement and good luck finding it. She's lucky I'm not actually here for that.

"You don't have to do this, Kitten." Alex says from directly behind me, his breath coming out in warm puffs against my neck. He'd spent the entire flight trying to dissuade me from confronting his parents, but there was also a light shining in his eyes every time I told him they can't treat him like that.

River's wearing a black wool coat with the collar popped up against the cold wind. December in Canada is several degrees cooler than it is in Boston.

He knocks on the door but doesn't smile when Mrs. Grayson opens it.

"River, I didn't know you were coming." Alex's mom says, genuine surprise in her voice. Her breath catches when she peers around him and spots Alex and I.

"You didn't mention you were coming too." She says to Alex.

I step forward, head held high, shoulders back and stride right to her. "Mrs. Grayson, is your husband home? I have something to say to both of you."

She swallows hard and her brows pinch together. It reminds me so much of Alex it's almost painful. "I'm not sure–"

"Just let us in, Mom."

She steps aside, and I walk past her. The house is comfortable. Orange-red floors that were all the rage in the early eighties. There's a brown suede sofa, with a knit blanket lying over the back. It reminds me of my grandma's house. I asked Alex if he ever sent them money and he heavily implied it was beneath them.

"George!" Mrs. Grayson practically shouts Alex's father's name, and he comes through the doorway and a genuine smile takes over his face.

"Alex, I didn't know you were coming."

"He's here because I asked him to come. I wanted to speak with you both about his celebration dinner."

Mr. Grayson glanced at his wife then back to me.

"I thought we already explained we can't come to that."

Any hope that it's just Alex's mom being the problem is squashed with those words.

Screw this. I square my shoulders and stare them down like Sidney taught me.

"Thank you for meeting me. I'm sorry for showing up here on false pretenses." I walk deeper in the room and the couple moves to stand beside each other, both looking weary. Good. They should be afraid of me. Alex and River stay at my back, never interrupting me, but I can feel their anticipation.

I don't look at them when I say, "I refuse to believe you don't love him the way I do. Not when he's not only sweet and kind, but determined and loyal. You raised an amazing son who puts his entire heart into everything he does. As his parents, you have to see that."

"Of course we do." His mother scoffs, and the hair on the back of my neck stands up.

Frustration courses through me. "Then go show him. Because all you've done up until now is show how proud of his brother you are, and he deserves to know that you're proud of him. I'm not going to pick apart why you've been acting so horribly because me getting even more pissed off isn't going to help anyone. You still have time to go fix it. Show him that you're proud of Who. He. Is." I punctuate each word with a point of my finger and keep going. "That you see how hard he's been working."

"Miss, I know you mean well, but Alex is an

athlete. A successful one, but we're an academic family. He showed great potential when he was younger and wasted it on hockey."

That's it. I hurl my words at them. "I can either help you appreciate him, or I can help him cut you ungrateful bitches out of his life because he *has* a family who loves him. Who will always be proud whether he's on the ice or not. We're proud of him because of who he is. He's not amazing because he's successful. He's successful because he's amazing. I refuse to believe you don't love him. Because how could you not? How could you not when I love him with every beat of my heart. Every breath I take. I expect to see you at that party. I expect you to show your oldest son as much love as you do your other. Because we're not putting up with this anymore." I toss down a piece of paper with the party's information on it, and spin only to be lifted into giant arms against a warm hard chest.

Alex walks us out of the house, my feet dangling off the ground as he squeezes me harder.

"I love you so much." his words rumble against me, and wool clad arms wrap around us both.

"I didn't overstep?" My nerves start to settle in now that the adrenaline has dissipated.

"Are you kidding me? That was so fucking hot." Alex bites the sensitive curve of my neck sending shivers down my back.

River hums. "I say fuck them. You two are all I've ever wanted, and we don't need them."

"Did you just wax poetically?" Even though I can't see him, I can hear the smile in Alex's voice.

"Only for you."

———

An hour later we're tucked onto the private plane. Instead of row upon row of seats there are four seats, two sets facing each other with a table in between at the front of the plane, and we're sitting on a long sofa at the back with a TV mounted on the wall. The interior is a dark gray, and screams guy vibes. I really need to ask River who his friend is.

Alex shifts, and his quads flex under my ass. I've been sitting on his lap since we got in here, I swear he hasn't let my feet hit the ground since we left his parents' house.

River's been watching us with a mix of heat and amusement at how his boyfriend's behaving. Alex moves again, and this time I feel the hard length of his cock pressed against my thigh. I rock my hips, drawing out a guttural moan from between his lips that encourages me to go further. I spin in his lap, straddling him. A hiss flows through my teeth as he perfectly aligns himself against my clit. His hooded gaze meets mine, and he leans in, capturing my mouth. His tongue is smooth, and soft, exploring every inch of my mouth. I hum, and he grips my ass, pressing me harder against his length, causing me to gasp.

"Right there." My words come out breathy, as I

search for the friction I need, but there are too many layers of clothing and I let out a frustrated grunt.

Alex laughs and bites my bottom lip lightly. "Feeling feisty?"

My skin is heated, and my core is throbbing with the need to be touched. "More like desperate."

A low rumble falls from his chest, and his mouth crashes over mine, devouring me in seconds.

River must have moved behind me, because his firm hands skirt below the hem of my shirt and at an achingly slow pace make their way up my sides, until his thumbs graze the sensitive skin below my breast.

"Have you ever wanted to be fucked on a plane, Love?" River's voice is dark and smoky and yanks on a cord that leads straight to my core.

"Not until now." I rasp and Alex chuckles against my mouth.

"That's my girl." River says, and backs away. I have to crane my head to see him. "I want you both naked." He points to me. "Then sit on his lap, your back against his chest. I want to eat my pussy."

I can hardly breathe as his words ricochet within me. I've never wanted anything so bad. Alex helps strip me down, before making quick work of his own. By the time I'm in position, River's standing in front of us. Shirt off, pants undone and cock in his hand. He's stroking it from root to head as he takes us in, sitting exactly how he told us. A sinister grin pulls up the corner of his lip, he likes the power he holds over us.

He drops to his knees and pushes mine, up and over the outside of Alex's, so I'm spread wide for him.

Dark eyes meet mine. "You were perfect today. Defending our family." His gaze dips between my thighs, where I'm already wet, and he trails his tongue over his teeth. "I think that deserves a treat. Don't you?"

Alex groans as I squirm in his lap, his cock pressed between us.

"Whatever you're thinking, River, I need you to do it now because I'm going to explode just sitting here with her." Alex says and rocks his cock into me with a grunt to prove his point.

River chuckles and brings his mouth just above where I'm aching for him, his soft breaths heating my clit. I have to force myself to not reach for his hair, and pull him into me, knowing that it'll just make him tease us longer.

I know what he wants. "Please. Please, River. Make us cum."

He growls, his control snapping, and his mouth is on me, tongue buried deep as he fucks it into me. He builds me up sucking, nipping, and licking but stops right before I break. Then he slows down, barely touching me and repeats until I'm soaking. My wetness coating my thighs and running down onto Alex's lap.

"Lift her up." River tells Alex, and he immediately complies. His cock escaping and bouncing forward, before coming back to slap against my clit.

My head tilts back with the impact and Alex settles me back down. With every rock of my hips, his cock strokes between my folds, driving me wild.

River watches where we're connected. "Fucking perfect." then dives down and mouths both of us.

"Fuck." Alex hisses the second the warmth of River's mouth envelopes us, driving me closer and closer to the edge. I can't get leverage in this position, and I give up trying to move, instead allowing Alex to manipulate my body, so that with each thrust, he drags against me and fits into River's mouth.

River doesn't stop licking us as he presses Alex's cock hard into my clit, rubbing it in circles. Tingles start in my spine and curve my hips, pulling a taut, aching knot between my thighs. "Please, please, please." I can't seem to say anything else, but it's enough.

Alex pulls back, then sinks his cock fully into me in one thrust. The stretch is both pleasure and pain, and I arch my back as my body accommodates him.

"That's it, Love. Look how good you take his cock." River says from where he's now standing, less than a foot from me. In our position, his cock is level with my mouth.

He rubs the tip along my lips, coating them in the salty taste of his pre-cum.

"Tongue out." He commands and I obey.

The weight of his cock lands on my tongue and pushes deep into my throat until I gag around it. He repeats the action and I struggle to keep my mouth open, but he hasn't told me to suck on him yet.

Alex follows River's tempo so that I sink onto his cock just as the head of River's cock rubs my tongue. They seesaw me between them, each fucking me their own way.

River's callused fingers wrap around my jaw, forcing it closed over him and groans as I suck him hard.

Alex shifts me so that my knees are beneath me, and gives me some control back. I'm able to fuck myself on him, while simultaneously taking River deep into my throat. The double penetration has my head swirling and I'm overcome with the needy sense for more. A whine slips from my lips and River pulls his cock out of my mouth with a pop.

I glare up at him.

"What do you need?"

When I just look at him.

He says, "I can tell you need something. Tell me what."

"I don't know. I need more." My voice sounds pained even to my ears. River fists my hair and slams his cock harder into my throat, giving me all of him. I have to swallow hard to fit him deep. Alex thrust up into me in a pounding rhythm, until my pulse rushes in my ears. It's still not enough. I still need more.

Alex palms my ass, then gently strokes his thumb over my hole and I know instantly that's exactly what I'm craving. I moan and rock between them, pushing back into Alex's hand.

He pushes his thumb deeper, and his voice comes

out in a low rumble. "You like that, don't you? You like us filling your every hole."

River grunts, and my orgasm slams into me as River's hot cum shoots down my throat. Alex doesn't slow. His thrusts turn rough as he chases his own release, and I have to brace my hands on River to stop myself from falling forward.

Alex comes on a growl, and he pulls my back against his chest and we both lay there, trying to catch our breaths.

River's panting in front of us and asks. "So how did you like joining the Mile High Club?"

CHAPTER 5
ALEX

TONIGHT'S the celebration dinner and nerves twist my stomach, wondering if my parents will make it. They looked genuinely embarrassed after Mia put them in their place, but they've had plenty of time to get over it.

All thoughts of them disappear when Mia steps out of the bedroom. My mouth drops open. It's a struggle not to pull her back inside. She's wearing a deep burgundy satin dress that skims all her curves, nipping in at the waist and flaring around her hips before stopping mid-thigh. She's left her hair down and it tumbles around her face in smooth curls, reminding me of a halo. She gives me a cheeky smirk, before spinning in place and showing off the smooth skin of her back, where her dress dips to just above her ass. I prowl forward and she turns toward me, anticipation written over her face. Fuck, we are never getting out of here.

Mia sucks in a breath when I close the distance between us in three easy strides.

She looks at me with round, green eyes and deep-red painted lips. Images of the red staining my cock has me crowding her against the wall, forcing her to tip her head all the way back to look at me.

"Do you like it?" she asks.

I dip my finger under the thin strap of her dress and run it along her shoulder, to where it connects at her chest. Goosebumps erupt under my touch, so I do it again. "You have no idea how much trouble I'm going to get into, taking you out in this."

She huffs out a breath. "Please don't tell me you're suddenly one of those guys that won't let their girlfriends dress how they want because they're jealous."

My gaze snaps to hers from where it had dropped to the perfect rounds of her tits. "Never." My lips pull up in a mischievous grin. "You can wear whatever you want, Kitten. I'm more than happy to fight any of my teammates that look at you too long."

Although I'm mostly kidding, there are a few guys on the team that I've never gotten along with and they better back the fuck off, or I'll be happy to give them incentive to.

She trails her fingers up my crisp black dress shirt, and circles each button as she makes her way to the open one near my neck. "Oh yeah?"

I swallow hard when her palms flatten on my chest and croak. "Yes."

She smirks, and I know in that second I'd give her

anything she asks. "Should I fight off every woman that looks at you?"

Running my thumb along her jaw, I tip her head back and let my lips graze hers. "Would you fight for me, Kitten?"

"Always."

"Well, aren't you two pretty?" River says after coming through the front door, from where he got changed across the hall. We've been using my apartment more like a giant walk-in closet since we've all moved into River's.

He shifts to lean back against the door, and loosely crosses his arms as he watches us. Mia steps to my side, and I throw my arm around her, tugging her closer as we all take each other in.

River's white dress shirt is perfectly tailored to show off a hint of his muscles. Enough to tease me with the idea of ripping it the fuck off him.

He straightens, standing to his full height, and crosses the room to us. He dips his mouth to mine, capturing it in a soft kiss, before doing the same with Mia. She sways on her feet, and I smile, steadying her.

River runs his thumb under her bottom lip, pulling it down slightly before stepping back. "I can't wait to see how they all drool over the two of you, and know that I'm the one that gets to take you home."

Holy shit.

My dick clenches painfully hard. "Let's stay home."

"It's your celebration party." Mia laughs.

"Exactly. It's my party and I can stay home if I want to."

She looks like she's considering it but River steps back.

"I have plans for you tonight and none of them involve a quickie on the way to the party.

"Come on, man." I protest at the same time my cock swells. I fucking love River's plans.

We somehow managed not to maul each other during the twenty-minute ride to the restaurant. Piper and Mia chose an Italian place that is known for both its food and ambiance. It's dimly lit, with thick drapery hung around the windows and large black chandeliers hanging from the ceiling.

The hostess eyes me, only to have River step between us. I give Mia a knowing glance and whisper. "So much for letting other people drool over us."

River turns toward me, his voice coming out as a warning. "Be good."

Fuck, I've never wanted to be bad as much as I do right now. To know exactly what River would do to us if we don't follow his orders. From the way Mia's looking at him, she's feeling the exact same way. She gives me a conspiratorial look before we follow the hostess into a private room at the back of the restaurant. My focus is on the low fabric of Mia's dress and how easy it would be to slip my hand under it and squeeze her ass. I follow after her like a puppy, completely oblivious to the stares around us.

"Congratulations!" The small space erupts in cheers and a giddiness bubbles in my chest. All of my teammates are here. Coach and assistant coaches all clapping as we enter. Pride takes over as I look around the smiling faces when I'm lifted off my feet.

"Fucking took you long enough." Jax laughs as he hauls me higher, earning him a disapproving grunt from River. He sets me down and grips my shoulder, turning serious. "All jokes aside. You deserve this."

"Move out of the way." Sidney's voice drifts up from where he's blocked her, and he moves immediately. I wonder if I look like that whenever Mia tells me what to do.

She smiles brightly and wraps me in a hug. "Congratulations."

Jax is quick to pull her back and wrap his hands around her middle, nuzzling his face into her neck. Whatever he says has her blushing.

I stumble back, and River's hand braces me as my mom and dad step into view. Their eyes dash around the room, both looking a little intimidated to be here.

"I wasn't sure you were coming." I pull my mom, then my dad in for a hug.

"Well, your girlfriend was very convincing," my mom replied.

Mia stands by my side, hands on her hips. "I'm glad you made it. I'll expect to see you both more often."

My dad clears his throat. "Of course."

She nods and gives them a genuine smile. "Good."

"Mia! Come sit up here." Piper cuts in from the other end of the long table where she and Lucas are standing. My parents take their seats at the other end. It's weird to have them here, but not a bad weird.

We make our way there, followed by a sea of congratulations, and Lucas slaps a hand on my back when I take the seat beside him. Mia next to me, and River on the other side of her.

Lucas leans in and whispers. "You should've been the captain in university. I'm happy someone finally smartened up and gave it to you."

I shake my head. "You needed it then. In hindsight, our college Coach was less of an asshole than I thought he was."

The room erupts with the sound of the guys chanting "Speech."

As the new captain I really should have expected this. I stand a little off balance and clear my throat.

"Well, would you look at this? Captain of the Boston freakin' Bruins! Can you believe it?"

One of my teammates shouts. "They ran out of options." and a laugh bursts out of me, killing any nerves I had.

"That's probably true. But hey, here we are, and I gotta say, it's an absolute honor. Thanks to the organization for trusting me with this C. I promise not to let it go to my head. Or maybe just a little."

"Big shoutout to the boys in the locker room. You guys are like my dysfunctional family, and I wouldn't want it any other way. To the rookies, welcome to the madhouse. You'll get used to the weird pre-game rituals and the strange superstitions. And, of course, to the vets, thanks for not scaring off the newbies too much."

"Coach, I don't know how you put up with us, but you do, and you do it well. I'm gonna try my best not to make your job any harder. Emphasis on "try.""

"And to the equipment guys, I'm sorry for all the times I've made you dig my lucky sock out of the laundry. I swear I'm working on my organizational skills. Not really, but I'll try. Now, let's fucking eat." I lift the glass of champagne that's in front of my plate and raise it.

"To the cup. We're coming for you."

A chorus of "To the cup." rings out, I take my seat.

Lucas leans over. "Nice speech."

"Thanks, buddy. Might've learned something from you."

There's rustling to my left and River stands holding his own glass. He looks over the table and quiet settles over us.

"I've been playing with Alex most of my career. He's always been the first to practice and the last to leave. He's the one that knows everyone's name and the small details I couldn't really give a shit about, like they're expecting a new baby and their kids' names."

River pauses as the guys laugh before continuing. "It's why he's going to be the best captain the Bruins have ever had. He has the biggest heart, and he's going to care about each and every one of you. You better fucking appreciate it. I have no problem laying any of you out on the ice."

There's more laughter, but the way Riv's looking at them, he's dead serious. He catches my gaze and speaks directly to me, sending butterflies fluttering in my chest. "Alex is one of the most important people to me. Take care of him."

One by one each player stands and says their own speech. Some long and others short. Lots of joking and teasing to go around. Jax told stories from university of what it was like to live with me and how he felt bad the team has to share a locker room with me. Lucas told the story about how he became captain, even though everyone knew it should've been me, and how much he appreciated that I supported him anyway. I whisper "fuck you" at him and he just laughs before sitting for the next person.

I couldn't help looking over at my parents, who are watching everyone with wide eyes. My mom turns to me and smiles. I smile back, not ready to completely forgive them for not being around, but happy it's a start.

Our food is here before the last person speaks and my stomach is rumbling as the smell of pasta fills my nose. Mia's small hand strokes my thigh closest to her and gives it a squeeze, pulling my attention off my plate and to her.

"I'm proud of you." She smiles and I fucking melt. I love this girl.

So I tell her. "I don't know what I'd do without you and River."

Her smile widens. "You'll never have to find out."

I move in and steal a kiss before she can stop me. She softens immediately and it's only the wolf whistles that have me pulling back. River raises a brow and I shrug. What? Like he isn't staring at her like a fucking snack.

I take a bite of pasta before I can kiss her again and moan around the mouthful.

River leans over Mia, so he can speak into my ear. "You keep making sounds like, that I'm taking you home."

Fuck, doesn't that send a thrill straight to my cock. So I take another bite, and moan louder, daring him to keep his promise.

He shakes his head and his gaze darkens in promise. Fuck, can we go yet?

Friendly chatter surrounds me as I eat. I look around and see all the people who are important to me in this room. Piper and Sidney laugh at whatever Jax and Lucas are shouting about. Both of the guys look at their girls with warm gazes, forgetting their argument. My heart swells, and I slide my hand down Mia's back, making her shiver.

Mia leans in close to me. "What are you doing?"

I drop my hand lower, dipping under the fabric to run my finger over the seam of her ass. She sucks in a breath, cheeks flushing pink. She looks delicious when she's riled up and all I want is to sit her on this table and eat my fucking dessert.

Her head tilts to the side, amusement tinted her voice. "Your parents are here."

"I don't care." I push my finger deeper and she squirms, red lips forming an O-shape. The image in my head of her splayed on the table with my mouth between her thighs changes to thoughts of her under the table, her warm lips wrapped around my cock.

"Alex." she half laughs half admonishes.

I rub the smooth skin of her ass, and give it a squeeze, leaning into her. "I fucking love this dress."

"We're going home." River practically growls at the two of us. His breath coming out in pants and his eyes pitch black, completely taken over by his pupils.

"It's early." I smirk. More than happy to go.

"Now." is his only reply.

The three of us stand and everyone gives us knowing looks as we announce our departure. I wave at my parents, not bothering to do formal goodbyes. I'm happy they showed up but everything isn't suddenly perfect. It is going to take time to rebuild the relationship, as they need to prove this wasn't a one-time thing. There's a few friendly jokes, but River doesn't give us time to respond. He pushes us out of the room, through the restaurant and to the car parked at the curb. He must have given them the heads up we were coming out.

"Alex." My head spins at the familiar voice. My brother is standing just outside the restaurant door. He looks nervous, his eyes darting all around before landing on me. "I'm glad I caught you."

"What are you doing here?"

"Her actually." He points at Mia. "Mom and dad

told me what she said." he takes a deep breath and straightens his shoulders. "I'm sorry, Alex. I should've been there for you. I should've made them be there for you." his voice turns more frustrated and sad. "I fucked up."

"It wasn't your job, it was theirs." I say.

He shakes his head. "No, it is my job. I'm your brother. I should have been there for you. I should have made sure they were too. I let my own bullshit get in the way of us. I'd like to fix that. If you're up to it."

"How?" Warmth fills my chest where hope builds.

"If you're okay with it, I want to come to your next game, and maybe we can hang out after?" He looks nervous.

"Yeah, I'd like that. I'll send you tickets."

"You don't have to–"

"First step of getting closer to Alex is letting him take care of you." Mia chimes in.

He nods. "Okay, then. I'm looking forward to it." He steps forward awkwardly, and I wrap him in a hug. I release him, giving him a nod and watch as he heads inside as we climb into the back of the town car. It's a tight fit, and I'm more than happy to pull Mia over my lap.

River gets in last and I ask, "You didn't step in?"

"You didn't need me." He brushes a strand of my hair off my forehead, and it falls back instantly. "If he wants a relationship with you, he's going to have to work for it. Just let me know if you want me to make that hard or easy on him." his voice is low...dark, and the unsaid promises make my blood pool lower.

With his touch, all thoughts of my brother vanish, and my attention is on the two of them.

I test my boundaries. "Was I good tonight?"

He shakes his head. "Not even a little bit."

I swallow. "What happens now?"

"You'll see."

The promise in his voice has my cock digging into Mia. The anticipation is going to kill me.

CHAPTER 6
RIVER

FUCK. The way Alex's eyes dilated at my promise has my dick pressing against the seam of my pants. He gives me a mischievous grin as he trails his finger along the thin strap of her dress. "I think if we're already getting punished, we should be extra naughty. Don't you, Kitten?"

"It's only fair." She arches into him, her nails digging into his thighs where she's draped over his lap.

He adjusts her so she's sideways, facing my way, with her back pressed into his half-turned chest.

I lean towards them, but she plants her heeled foot against my chest, holding me in place. The already short hem pools low around her ass, revealing sheer black panties.

A growl forms in my throat. "Now, Mia. You don't really want to start this, do you?"

"I don't know what you're talking about." She

says innocently, leaving her foot planted firmly in place.

Alex guides the straps of Mia's dress over her shoulders, so that the neckline slips down her breast, catching on the peak of her nipples. The fabric threatens to fall with each of her breaths, and my mouth waters with the need to taste them.

I go to pry her foot away, but she shakes her head at me.

She bites her lip. "Not yet."

"You don't give me orders."

She lifts one perfect brow. "Give up control for one night."

She's temptation incarnate. I want to dominate her, and show her who's in charge, but an equal part of me wants to see where this is going. I want to let them have their fun.

"Isn't our girl perfect?" Alex asks in a low rumble. His hands trail up her ribs until his thumbs gently brush the lower curve of her breast.

"Yes." I breathe.

The driver clears his throat and I meet his eyes in the rear-view mirror. There's an unmistakable warning in my gaze and he immediately looks forward.

"We have an audience." I watch Alex and Mia for signs of being uncomfortable, but if anything, they look more turned on. I relax back, taking her calf in my hand, and giving it a little squeeze letting her know I'll play nice. For now. "Show me."

Alex tugs on the silk and it slips free of her chest,

revealing two perfectly pink nipples. I grip the seat to stop myself from moving, and watch Alex's hands cup her full breasts, raising them, then pressing them together. The visual has me picturing fucking her pretty tits while Alex holds them for me.

Mia lifts her hands and buries them in Alex's hair as he circles her taut peaks. She's rolling her hips, pressing herself against him, in nothing but that slip of a dress looped around her hips.

My hand on her calf, slides higher, so that it's hitched behind her knee and I pull it wider giving me the perfect view of her pussy.

"Get her naked for me." I can't stop the command.

The car jerks and Mia makes a pained sound.

"What the fuck?" There's nothing playful about Alex's tone.

"Sorry." The driver squeaks out, but doesn't turn back to look at us. He's faced his rearview mirror to the side so I know he can't see us, but he's obviously listening.

Mia just grins like the cat that ate the canary and lifts her hips, sliding off her panties before giving them to me to slip into my pocket. "Like that?"

"Just like that, Love." I kiss the side of her knee, nibbling higher to see how far she'll let me.

Alex slides his hands up her thighs spreading her further, showing off her soaking pussy. She freezes, barely breathing as he moves to her core.

Breathe, Love. I say silently in my head.

All three of us groan when Alex sinks his fingers

into her, pumping them in and out in a slow, purposeful rhythm. Her hips swirl, chasing his hand and soft gasps fall from her mouth. Our girl is already close and we're just getting started.

A small whimper escapes her when he pulls his fingers out. Even in the dark, I can see they're glistening.

He leans forward, running them along my bottom lip. "Suck."

A low growl rumbles my chest, and I suck him hard. Her sweet taste fills my mouth. I let my jaw close, my teeth scraping along Alex's fingers as he pulls them out.

He groans. Grasping my jaw. "Not fair."

"Fuck. Fair."

That must be the right answer, because he rakes his fist into Mia's hair, tipping her head back, and captures her mouth in his. "I want to see you take his cock. Will you do that for me, Mia?"

My cock aches as I watch Mia process his question. She glances toward the driver who's diligently not watching, then nods.

I rip at my belt and pants, popping a button in my haste, and push them to my thighs. I climb over them. Placing one hand on the window at Alex's back and the other on his shoulder. Alex immediately grabs my cock, wiping the precum from the tip and feeding it to Mia. Her pink tongue runs along the pad of his thumb and she moans around it.

He pulls me forward by my cock, lining me up perfectly with her pussy. Mia's panting, looking up at me. I capture her mouth with mine. She's sweet, soft, smooth, and delicate as I control the kiss.

I sink into her, inch by inch, letting her adjust to my size. Then rock in slow controlled movements, as her warm pussy clenches around me.

Strong fingers grip in my hair and Alex rips my head back. His hooded gaze on mine. "Look how good you fill her. Stretching her wide around your cock."

My hips jerk, and my movements lose their control, as I pound into her. Alex reaches between us, rolling and pinching her nipple with one hand and the other massages her clit. Her cries turn desperate as she writhes against my cock and his hand.

She pulses around me, squeezing me until my breath freezes in my chest, and I forget my own name as I fill her with my cum.

Fuck. I collapse against them, breath ragged, as I try to gain some sense of control.

I lift my head, and check on Mia. Her eyes are closed, and there's a soft upturned tilt to her lips. I kiss her forehead before pulling back, my cum dripping from her. Alex catches it with his hands and stuffs it back into her. My mouth grows dry, and I track his motions as he brings his fingers to his mouth and licks me off of them.

It's only when Mia giggles, I realize we've stopped. Our driver is out of the car. No doubt giving us a minute to get our shit together. I grab my coat and help Mia into it. She's looking at me with a dopey smile.

"What's with you two and cars?"

I laugh. "It's not the car, it's you. It takes too long to get you home."

Alex gets out first, followed by Mia. I use the added space to adjust myself so I'm put together before stepping out. Alex already has Mia inside the building. My coat's so long on her you wouldn't know that the only thing she's wearing is a thin slip of fabric bunched around her hips.

I stalk them through the lobby. The second we get into the elevator, I'm going to watch him fuck her raw until she's filled with both of our cum.

The doors open and we step in. I crowd into Alex, and I can hear his breath hitch when I run my teeth along the shell of his ear and grip his cock through his pants. "Is this your game tonight? Do you want to play being in charge?"

We both know I'm the one who really is.

"I want you to feel like you make me feel."

The air is knocked out of me, and I meet his soft eyes.

I nod.

"Happy holidays." Two middle aged ladies with small dogs in their arms, step inside seconds before the doors close.

"Happy holidays. Having a good night?" Mia asks, giving them a bright smile.

I unwrap my hand from Alex's length and let my head fall back against the mirrored wall. Of course the ladies don't get off until the floor below us. I consider hitting the emergency stop, but a quick glance at the cameras tells me the car was enough of a show for today.

Alex lifts Mia off the ground, letting me pass to open the door.

The apartment is dark, only the moon shining from the floor-to-ceiling windows illuminating the space.

I go to flip the switch, but Alex stops me. "Leave it."

I let my hand drop and follow him into our place, where he gently slides Mia's feet to the ground. She lets my coat slip off her shoulders and shimmies the rest of the way out of her dress. She's looking at us in anticipation, standing naked in just her stiletto heels.

How the hell did I get this lucky?

He strokes his thumb along her jaw and cups the back of her neck. "I'm going to fuck your pretty little mouth. Kneel." His voice is low, pure command and she drops instantly.

Those bright green eyes, shining up at him, are nearly my undoing. Mia's sitting back on her ankles, hands resting on her thighs, just waiting for what Alex tells her to do next. I fight back the urge to take over and wait for Alex instead.

"Take my cock out."

My dick hardens with his words, and I watch our girl undo his pants, pulling him out. He's huge in her hand, thick and long, pre-cum pooling at the tip.

"Suck."

Mia takes him deep into the back of her mouth, before pulling back and rolling her tongue over his tip and pushing back down. Alex rakes his fingers into her hair, guiding her deeper, forcing her to take more of him into her throat. He reaches for me, burying his hand in my pants and grips my cock hard.

I grunt, his touch verging on pain, and rock into his fist, following the pace he sets with Mia. He yanks her head back, and she watches him with wide eyes.

"Suck on him."

Within seconds Mia's warm, wet mouth wraps around my cock, and Alex pumps me harder. The two of them push me closer to the edge. Tingles start in my spine, traveling down my thighs, tightening my balls. "Fuck. I'm going to come."

Alex rips her off me, leaving me panting.

"Did I tell you, you can come?"

The corner of my mouth tips up. "No."

"Your orgasm is mine. I want you to feel our girl wrapped around your cock as I take your virgin ass." He slaps me. "Because you are a virgin for me, aren't you, Baby?"

My dick bobs, cum leaking from the tip as a thrill shoots down my body. His light brown eyes are serious on mine. He wants to fuck me, wants to take control. My words are caught in my throat, lust taking over, but I manage to rasp my approval.

"Good boy."

Fuck me. My eyes roll back. He's killing me using my words against me.

"Where do you want me?" Mia asks, and Alex

lifts her from the ground and sits her on the table, gently pressing her shoulder until she lays back.

"Don't move, Mia. Will you be good for me?"

She grips the table edges. "Yes."

He rewards her by licking up her cunt. Her hips buck forward, and he bites her hip bone. "You're moving."

"Sorry." She says breathlessly.

He trails his thumb along her seam, coating it in her wetness, before circling her clit. Her fingers turn white where they grip the table, but she doesn't move.

"That's our girl. Listening so well." He buries his mouth between her legs, devouring her, the sloppy sounds indecent.

He's enjoying telling us what to do. Images of having him tied up, pushed over the chair, my cock deep in his ass, while I spank him raw fill my mind. I'll let him have his fun for now.

"Taste her." Alex commands.

I grip Mia's left leg, spreading her further apart, and place my mouth beside Alex's. His spit mixes with mine as we eat her. Her desperate cries fill my ears, and I curl two fingers inside her pussy, pressing her g-spot while Alex works her clit. She breaks apart on a cry, screaming our names, her core pulsing around my fingers.

I hum and kiss the tender spot between her hip and thigh, giving her time to calm down before lifting to stand.

Alex is there, his mouth on mine, taking me in a

hungry kiss. He thrust his tongue to the back of my throat, fucking it into my mouth as we rip the remainder of each other's clothes off. My heart's pounding in my chest, knowing what's next. He drops his forehead to mine, his breaths fanning over my lips, and places his palm over my heart. "I've got you."

My body relaxes, and I give myself over. "I know."

He smirks. "Good. Now, go fuck our girl."

Mia's propped up on one elbow, her other hand working her clit slowly while her gaze is hot on Alex and I. She's so perfect for us, it almost hurts.

I grip her ankles, guiding them back so her knees are fully bent, then pull her down so her ass is hanging over the table. I fill her in one smooth movement, knowing she doesn't need time to adjust. She's so wet, she's dripping down my cock with each thrust.

I vaguely notice Alex leaving the room, too consumed with our girl to care.

Her pussy's gripping me, pulling me deeper with each pump.

Alex presses against my back, his length slotted between my cheeks and I stiffen. He runs his nose along my neck, and sucks the lobe of my ear into his mouth. "Breathe, River. I'm going to make this feel good."

My hips jerk forward, filling Mia to the hilt and my fingers dig into her thighs hard as I wait for his touch.

Cool liquid trails down my crack, and I moan as Alex circles it against my hole. I've used toys before, but this is something else. Something more.

He presses in, first one finger, working it in and out a few times before adding another. The double sensations of her wet pussy and his thick fingers almost too much. Not enough.

He strokes me a few more times, before pulling back and replacing his fingers with a cool metal. My eyes roll back as he pushes it into my ass, carefully fucking me with it until I can't stop myself from grind against it, needing more.

He pulls it out. "You're perfectly needy for my cock."

I groan as his blunt tip circles my hole. He feels huge against my ass, and I tighten.

Alex coos into my ear, and he massages my hip with his hand until I relax into his touch. He presses firmly until the head of his cock breaches my tight rim. I groan against the burn, but I want him so fucking bad I don't care.

I shift back, taking more of him in and he chuckles. "You can't give up control, can you?"

Thrusting against him, pushing him in deeper, I grind out. "No."

My eyes roll into the back of my head as he hits my prostate, and my world goes white before coming back to focus. Mia's rocking herself on me, squeezing around my cock while Alex takes my ass.

He shifts faster, like he can't help himself and groans. "Fuuuck. Your ass feels so good, taking me deep. You want me to fill you with my cum? Want to be dripping with me?"

"*Fuck*." I cry out, as my orgasm nearly crests. "Yes. Fuck yes."

He bites my shoulder, pain grounding me from the intense pleasure as he fucks me into Mia. I hold her in place, marveling at the feel of them both. She's stunning, her chest flushed pink, fingers pinching her nipples, while her other hand rubs her clit. Her eyes don't leave mine as her orgasm takes over, pussy pulsing around me, pulling me after her.

Alex groans, his teeth sinking deeper into my flesh, as I clench around him. Hot cum spurts in my ass as he finishes with jerky movements.

I collapse, face resting against Mia's chest, gulping for breath as my heart pounds out of my chest. Shivers rack through my body with the after-shocks of my orgasm.

Alex carefully pulls out of me, rubbing his palm up my back. "Are you okay?"

His touch and voice are tender, and I nod. "So much more than okay."

I lift my chin, resting it on Mia's breastbone and she smiles at me.

"That was hot."

"Somehow the two of you got out of your punishment."

Her smile widens. "You're easily distractible."

"Is that right?" I growl, nipping at her breast, and she wiggles underneath me.

"Yes." She laughs and tries to escape my touch, my fingers finding their way over her sensitive ribs.

I tickle her. "Tell me you love me."

"I love you. I love you. I love you." She's full-on squirming by the time I finally let her go.

I lean over capturing her mouth. "I love you too."

Alex's hand wraps around my throat, tugging my back to his chest, and his lips graze my ear. "Do you love me too?"

"Always."

CHAPTER 7
ALEX

MIA MOANS in her sleep and goosebumps erupt over her skin as I slowly kiss my way up the inside of her thigh. Her legs part for me naturally, making room for my wide shoulders and I press my nose into her pussy, breathing deeply before licking her from ass to clit. She stirs awake, stuttering and her fist goes into my hair, tugging it tight. I groan as her sweet taste fills my mouth and sink my tongue into her center. She moans my name and my eyes meet hers.

I give her a cocky smile. "Morning kitten."

"Morning." She says in a raspy voice.

I love the way her cheeks pinken with each lick of my tongue. I lift her thigh above my shoulder, spreading her wider and go back to fucking her with my tongue. I move faster as her hips rock against my face and follow the tempo that she sets.

I replace my tongue with my fingers and thrust two deep inside of her while capturing her clit and flick the sensitive spot with my tongue repeatedly, listening to her moan over and over. I flatten my tongue against her clit, rubbing it hard in slow, deliberate circles. Mia's thighs clamp around my head, holding me in place as her entire body trembles with the force of her orgasm. She screams my name as I lick her through wave after wave of her release.

"Alex." she hums, not quite ready for words.

Turning my head, I kiss along her smooth thigh before biting gently. She squirms underneath my touch, tugging on my hair and I chuckle. Slowly, I work my way up her body, kissing her stomach, over her navel, her breast, her collarbone and up her neck, nipping her ear before kissing her temple.

"Well, that's one way to wake up." Her voice is still raspy.

I smile into the curve of her neck and let my cock press against her core, loving the way she bucks against it.

"Best." I kiss her smooth skin. "Breakfast." Trail my nose higher and nip the bottom of her ear. "Ever."

She rakes her nails down my spine and then gently grazes my ass.

"I could get used to this." She says.

A smile takes over my face, knowing I'm more than happy to do this every morning. I lift my head and meet her smiling face and capture her mouth, letting my tongue show her everything I'm feeling.

I hold my weight with one hand beside her head, then dig my free hand into her hair and tilt her head up so I can thrust my tongue deeper into her mouth. She moans as I sink my cock into her pussy. She's wet and warm and tight, everything I've ever wanted. I thrust hard, driving her into the mattress with each press of my hips.

I imprint the feel of her...of us... into my memory into my bones with each thrust.

Until all I think about is them. Dream about, taste, feel. Every time I close my eyes, all I see is the two of them laid out for me.

I work my hips in deep, slow thrusts, driving us both crazy. I drop my forehead to hers, meeting her green gaze and shutter when she tightens around my cock.

After last night, you'd think I would last longer, but the second her walls clench around me and she trembles in my arms, I come with her. A guttural groan escaping my lips with my release.

Mia's eyes lose focus and I watch her from above. As the light from the wall-to-wall windows dances across her face, highlighting the smooth slope of her nose and the plump bow of her lips.

I'm still catching my breath when her gaze clears and she looks beside us.

"Well, you two had a good morning." River says from the doorway and I'm just about to make a comment about him joining us when my eyes focus on his outfit, and I bust out laughing. "What the fuck?"

Our usually perfectly styled River is wearing a red Christmas sweater with a fucking elf on it, and matching candy cane print pyjama pants.

"Oh my God." Mia says between laughter.

"Glad you like them. I got you a set." He tosses us each a box wrapped in shiny Christmas paper.

Mia dives into her package. She hasn't stopped giggling since she spotted him, and the light sound fills the room.

Sure enough, I find a sweater and sleep pants in my present, but instead of an elf, mine has a snowman. There's a childish, silliness to the whole thing. Nothing about this reminds me of River.

I go to make a smart-ass comment when I see him. River's eyes are warm, cheeks tinged a light pink, and he's smiling as he watches Mia pull her sweater over her head. He looks so fucking happy that my eyes burn, and I have to cover it by pulling my own sweater on.

"How do I look?" I ask cheekily, because I definitely look like an idiot.

"Perfect." River answers easily. Like it's no big deal to be throwing out compliments my way. The way he talks to me when we fuck is one thing, but now. Now he has me feeling warm and glowy all day long.

Just as I'm picturing stripping him out of his adorable fucking pants, I hear a small bell come from the doorway.

Crookshanks sits glaring at us, wearing a tiny matching sweater with the arms cut out.

Mia covers her mouth. "You didn't?"

"I did." River says it matters a fact.

I search River, sure he's been shredded by the cat's claws. "Do I need to call a medic?"

River's dark gaze. "He and I have a deal."

"Tell me you didn't give him more treats!" Mia panics beside me. "He's supposed to be on a diet."

River and Crookshanks look at each other, like the cat can actually fucking think. "I'd rather not lie to you."

Her eyes narrow on him for several seconds before her mouth cracks into a smile. "He cuddled you and you caved, didn't you?"

"You'll never know. Now come on, I have something else for you in the living room."

I jolt upright. "I thought we weren't exchanging presents until Christmas day? Today's just friends' Christmas."

"Not a Christmas present. Now, both of you finish getting dressed before I cave and you don't leave the bed all day."

Mia and I share a conspiratorial glance because that sounded entirely too appealing.

"Sidney, Jax, Piper, Lucas. Remember, they're all waiting for us." River calls over his shoulder as he exits the room.

"Fine." I help Mia up, and follow her, pulling her onto my lap on the couch.

River stands above us, looking ridiculous in his outfit. My smile is cut off when he drops to one knee in front of us, his expression dead serious and holds out a box to Mia.

She sucks in a breath. Her body practically vibrates in anticipation as he slowly opens it, revealing a thin silver band. She reaches for it and he clamps the lid shut.

"Mia, I know nothing about us is traditional and you've mentioned not wanting to get married, but I'm hoping you'll take my ring and accept me as one of your partners for life."

"Yes." She practically screams it, and jumps into his arms, nearly knocking them both over as she kisses him.

My chest is warm, happiness bubbling under my ribs, but there's also a darker worrying feeling in my gut. One that I've never had with them until now. I clamp it down. They deserve this moment.

"I'll just grab us coffees." I start to stand giving them space, but River grips my hand and squeezes.

"Stay." he says, and gently lifts Mia off his lap so she's sitting on the floor beside him.

I drop back down, fighting against the uncomfortable feeling of imbalance I know I need to get over. I look toward the door. I just want to get out of this fucking room.

"Alex." River's tone is soft, and pulls my attention back to him. He's holding another small box and my heart's about to pound out of my chest, as what's happening slams into me. "I've always known you'd be my best friend, but will you be my partner for life too?"

I reach down, grab the collar of his ridiculous sweater and haul him up to me. "Fuck, I love you."

I kiss him hard, and all feeling of inadequacy erases from my body. River lets me control the kiss for several seconds, then takes over. He strokes his tongue deep into my mouth before sucking mine into his. I groan and he pulls off, giving me a soft smile.

"Was that a yes?" he asks.

"It's a fuck yes." I say stealing another kiss, before he pulls away.

"Um…" Mia shifts. "What about you? I want you to wear a ring."

The idea of them both wearing my ring sends a thrill through me.

"I want that too. Which is why I took the liberty of having a third band made." He holds up his left hand and sure enough, there's a silver band circling his ring finger.

"That's fucking hot." I say and Mia agrees.

"Agreed." River says, his voice dark. "Now put yours on."

I lift my ring from its box delicately. It's slightly wider than Mia's but looks identical to River's. The light catches on a small engraving.

Yours, Mine, Ours

CHAPTER 8
MIA

WE PULL into Lucas and Piper's neighborhood, snow crunching under our tires, and my mouth falls open. We haven't been back since this summer's Prosthetics For Kids kickoff event and I wasn't prepared for how pretty the streets would look, lined with last night's heavy snowfall. Rooftops lined with powder and icicles hanging from eaves; the morning sun sparkles off everything. We aren't far from the city center, but with one turn onto their street, the world has been transformed into a magical Winter Wonderland.

You'd think, with the architecture varying with each home, it would be a visual disaster, but some-how, having a modern traditional house next door to a craftsman works here. I gaze through open windows as we pass by, imagining one of these places is ours.

Up ahead there's a for sale sign and I'm leaning so far forward my nose touches the cool window.

"See something you like, Love?" I lean away from the door and shrug.

"Just daydreaming. It's stunning here."

River tilts his head, scanning my face. "It is."

We drive past the house for sale, and my breath catches in my throat. It's modern and organic and it reminds me so much of Napa that my heart squeezes in my chest. We don't have a reason to move. River's apartment is more than enough for the three of us. When you add in Alex's, it's almost too much, but I don't look away as we drive by, instead swiveling in my seat to get one last look.

Alex turns into Lucas and Piper's driveway. Their home is a stunning two-level with taupe siding and a wrap around porch. Their Christmas lights are buried beneath snow, giving the powder a multi-color shine.

Alex opens my door, his smile taking over his whole face and holds out his hand to me. He adjusts my beanie on my head, covering my ears. "You look all bright-eyed and bushy-tailed."

I shrug, then take his hand, letting him guide me out. "It's just so freaking pretty." I take one step and my Ugg's slip on the ice-covered ground, sending me backward.

Strong arms grasp me from behind. "Easy there."

River's cedar and leather scent fills my nose and I lean into his warmth. "I may be a little clumsy."

"A little?" Alex laughs. He's holding several bags, filled with the presents we brought for everyone.

Have I been known to walk into random things,

and trip on imaginary objects? Sure. Will I admit that to anyone? Absolutely not. "Yes, just *a little*. I'm mostly limber and well balanced."

"Good, Love. We'll test you on that later."

Heat rushes between my thighs, and my knees go weak. River tightens an arm around me to keep me steady. He buries his face in my hair, and growls into my neck. "You may not be clumsy, but you're definitely dangerous."

His voice sends a shiver dashing through me that has nothing to do with the cold.

Our attention is pulled away when the front door swings open, revealing Piper and Lucas milliseconds before I decide to say screw it and make up an excuse to go home.

"Too late, Love." River's lips graze my skin before he leans away. He guides me toward the house, keeping a firm grip on my arm, just in case I slip again. It feels a little overprotective, but I'm here for it.

It's not until I get closer to them that I realize Lucas and Piper have matching plaid onesies on and I spiral into giggles.

"Where did you even find one that would fit you, man?" Alex asks Lucas.

"Easy." Piper answers. "I had them custom made."

The vibration from River's laugh travels through my arm, and I give him a little squeeze.

"What are you laughing at?" Lucas demands, then does a spin revealing a little butt flap panel at the back, that's buttoned in place. "I look good. You on the other hand have a fucking elf on your sweater."

I shake my head. "It's not a competition, guys."

All three men look at me with raised brows.

"Alright…maybe everything is."

Piper takes pity on me and shoves Lucas aside so we can enter. Their place is stunning, large open windows let the sun fill the space with a warm glow, but it's the Christmas decorations that have me grinning like a little kid. The entire place is covered with decorations. Garland, ornaments, and lights decorating every surface. I spin and my mouth drops open.

"Holy crap, they have three trees."

"You okay, Kitten? You look a little…excited."

I turn wide eyes on him and whisper-yell. "They have *three* trees."

Alex leans toward me. "Fuck, you're cute." then kisses me. It starts soft and simple, but quickly grows heated.

"There will be no kissing between you three until after breakfast. I don't want to lose my appetite." Jax's familiar voice cuts in and I pull away from Alex to smile up at him.

"I'll remember that." Alex says, his tone full of amusement and fake anger.

I hear Sidney say, "Move out of the way." right before I'm wrapped in her arms.

Pulling her close, I hug her tight. "I missed you!"

She looks me over, then grabs my hand and her mouth drops open. "Oh. My. God."

I chuckle, as everyone around us realizes we have matching bands.

"Did you get married without us?" Piper asks incredulously.

I freeze, having no idea how to answer that when River does it for me. "We're committed for life, the rings are just a visual way to let everyone else know we're off limits."

"Congratulations!" Sidney wraps me in a hug, then points to the kitchen. "Come on. They've got mimosas and pastries!"

Their place smells like a bakery, a mix of cinnamon, apples, and lemon. The second I turn the corner and see their island, I understand why. Every inch of the car length marble slab is covered in some form of baked goods. Pies, rolls, buns, freaking muffins.

Sidney grabs a flakey croissant and when she breaks it open, there's warm chocolaty goo inside. "This is my third one. *So good.*"

I go for a scone, sniffing blueberry and lemon, then grab a glass of bubbly orange mimosa. I have a feeling the next few hours are going to be intense with all of them. My plate is lifted from my hands.

River stands to my right, adding more to the plate, picking and choosing the desserts until he's satisfied.

I look at the heaping plate. "Did you get one of everything?"

"I wanted to make sure you and Alex have

options for when you want more." He says it so easily. Like, of course he'd go out of his way to make sure his boyfriend and I have extra food. As if it's not one of the sweetest things he does, and he doesn't even realize he's doing it. Hell, if you ask him, I guarantee he'd tell you it's his pleasure to take care of us.

I wrap my arms around his neck, startling him, and lift on my toes, closing the distance between our mouths. I smile against his lips when the kiss slows down. "I love you, River Jonathon Davis. You are amazing, and I am madly in love with you."

His cheeks turn that perfect shade of pink. "It's just food."

I shake my head no. "It's so much more. You are so much more than I ever thought I would deserve."

"What are you saying to our boyfriend to make him blush like that?" Alex comes up behind River, and kisses his temple. The moment is painfully sweet.

"Just that I think he's perfect and we're lucky to have him."

Alex grabs a muffin from the plate and takes a bite. "All facts."

The two of them walk into the living room to hang out with Jax and Lucas. Alex is smiling wide at something Jax has said, and warmth builds in my stomach. Everything feels so right. I'm feeling all sappy when Sidney and Piper flank my sides watching the guys with me.

"How did we get so lucky?" Piper asks. Lucas

looks over, giving her a soft look before returning his attention to the guys.

I take a sip of my mimosa. "It wasn't easy."

"Nothing worth it ever is." Sidney adds right before the guys beckon us over.

———

We spend the next hour eating and catching up with our friends. We see Piper and Lucas all the time, since we all work together, but with Jax and Sidney living in Ottawa, we are rarely all together. So when we are, our time is filled with laughing, bickering and catching up. Sometimes I forget that Piper, Lucas and Jax grew up together, but the second they're in the same room, it's clear as day how close they are. I rest my head on River's shoulder. I'm sandwiched between him and Alex on the couch, facing our friends.

He runs his fingers through my hair, and between the soothing motion and my extremely full stomach, I feel ready to pass out.

Lucas heads to the kitchen and comes back with an actual freaking serving tray, handing us all a drink. It's a weird purplish mauve color.

"It's something I'm working on. I call it Purple Swirl." Lucas answers without me having to ask.

I take mine, bringing it under my nose and the little pops of bubbles tells me it's champagne based. He hands Piper her drink last and I can't help but notice it looks a little different. The purple is more saturated and it doesn't have the bubbles mine does.

Before I can ask about it, Lucas holds up his drink. "Toast to you. The best family I could ask for. Even if you're all a pain in my ass."

"You should've told me it hurt, man. I'd have been more gentle." Alex chimes in fake innocently and I snort my drink up my nose.

Lucas's brown skin is tinged pink as he gawks at Alex. "This is why we can't have nice things."

Alex leans in and rests the side of his head against mine. "I don't know, I think we're doing alright."

A grinning Sidney, who's laughing so hard there's tears in her eyes, tries to calm herself down enough to speak. "Okay. Lovely toast. Let's do presents."

She reaches down and grabs a bag, passing one to each of us.

I pull out a small rectangle, instantly identifying it as a book and smile when I peel the paper. It's filled with pictures of us, and my eyes burn as I flip through page after page of us together.

She sniffs. "I wanted to give you all something so you know that even though Jax and I live a country away, you still have us with you."

"And that's why I got you these." Jax cuts through the seriousness and tosses us all a small package. Lucas is the first to open his and his laughter has me tearing through mine.

Boxers. Specifically, underwear with Jax's face on it.

Sidney sees what he gave us and snaps her attention his way. He raises both hands up. "Trouble. You said give them something to remember me by and I did." He drops his face close to her ear and I can just make out his words that have her turning crimson. "You like it when my face is on you–"

"I'll wear them all the time. Thank you, Jax." I hold them up to get a good look at them, only to have them ripped away. River's collected all three of our pairs and shoved them in a bag.

At the look of my disappointment, River strokes his thumb over my cheek. "Sorry, Love. But we don't share."

"Are you always going to be jealous and possessive?"

"Yes. Is that going to be a problem?" His voice is a purr and warmth builds low in my stomach.

"No." My response is a little squeaky, earning me one of his dark grins.

"Okay…who's next." Lucas calls out and Alex grabs the bags we brought and passes them out.

Piper and Sidney unwrap theirs first. We got them rink bags filled with a seat warmer, a long, warm blanket and a charging pack for their phones. River made me one and it's been a freaking godsend.

The guys picked out Lucas's gift. Some kind of hockey thing they swore he'd like and he seems happy, but it's Jax's reaction that we're waiting for.

The guys triple wrapped his, so everyone's watching as he finally gets it open.

"You fuckers." Jax huffs out a laugh, holding up a miniature replica of the Stanley cup.

"River and I figured it's the only way you'll ever get one, so we wanted it to be from us."

The pillow Jax whips at Alex goes wide, and I brace for the impact that never comes. River caught it inches from my face and the glare he's gives Jax has the over six-foot forward squirming in his seat.

"Sorry, Mia." He gives me a signature Jax grins, with dimples and all.

"You're lucky my best friend loves you." I reply playfully.

His smile widens, and he looks all lovey. "I really fucking am."

Piper stands, putting down her barely touched drink. "That leaves us. Wait until everyone has theirs. I want you all to unwrap them together."

She and Lucas hand out the boxes, wrapped in gold. She's watching Jax, who's looking at her with his head tilted.

"On the count of three. One. Two. Three." I swear any countdown is a competition with these guys and the second she said the last number it was a race to who could open theirs first.

The paper rips apart revealing a light blue t-shirt. My brows pinch together when I see what's written on it. *Auntie.*

Alex and River both have ones that say uncle, but it's Jax that I'm watching. He stands and goes to Piper. She pulls her onesie tight showing off a small baby bump. Jax's eyes dart over her, seeing the truth.

"Pips? Are you pregnant?" There something entirely too sweet about seeing these giant hockey

RULES WE BREAK   95

guys turn into actual goo. He's holding his hands out like he's afraid to touch her.

"Yes." Piper's laugh is watery and she wraps her arms around the guy who'd been like a second big brother to her.

She pulls back, tears in her eyes. "We're naming him, Marcus."

SNEAK PEEK

Keep reading for the steamy, kick your feet in the air inducing, heartfelt, college hockey romance, Rule Number Five.
Available on Amazon at https://amzn.to/40pYmvt

RULE BREAKER SERIES

RULE NUMBER FIVE

Five rules for dating a hockey player

Rules

USA TODAY BESTSELLING AUTHOR

J. WILDER

RULE NUMBER FIVE

JAX

"You've got to be fucking kidding me, man."

Alex met my gaze across the table and grinned, showing off the lipstick smeared on his cheek. He'd been practically fucking a redhead in our booth for the last fifteen minutes, and her moans had officially reached soap-opera-acting level of ridiculous. Not that I minded if a girl wanted to get laid, but that wasn't a puck bunny's MO. They were out to catch a free ride and didn't give a single shit if they liked you or not. A shiver crawled down my spine. It made me feel used and dirty. I had to get the hell out of there before he convinced her to get on her knees beneath us.

Not that I expected anything less. Alex had always been a bit of a puck slut.

He gave me an unapologetic shrug but disentangled himself, dropping her feet to the floor, then smacked her ass. "How about you get us a beer, sweetheart?"

"How about you come with me?" Even though we all knew she would do it anyway, she still pouted when he just stared at her. With one last look, her shoulders dropped, and she walked off in a huff toward the bar.

The club was in a warehouse with giant concrete pillars that divided the space and multicolored strobe lights pulsing over a dance floor. On the furthest side, there was a long glass bar serving every type of drink you could think of.

"She's going to spit in your beer," I said with a grin wide enough that I knew my dimple was showing and raked my hand through my messy brown hair.

Alex laughed. "Eh, never know. I might like it."

"Alright, fucker." Standing, I grabbed my coat from the booth. "I'm out before she comes back with friends."

"Hey, you're supposed to be my wingman," he argued.

"If I wanted to catch bunnies, I'd have stayed at the rink." Sure, I was down when he asked, still high off our win, but I wasn't interested in these girls.

"Fucking picky bastard. Hold up," Alex grumbled under his breath and searched the crowd before a slow smile formed on his lips. Then he gestured toward the other side of the club with his chin. "How about them?"

I followed his gaze to a girl at a bar-height table.

She was tall, blonde, and had a deep tan that gave her a sun-kissed look. By the way Alex looked at her, she must've been his type, but I was too blindsided by the hot-as-fuck brunette standing beside her to notice.

"Fuck me," I said low under my breath as I took in the brunette. She looked like some kind of sexy librarian, wearing a short pleated skirt, thigh-high socks, and chunky black boots. She smiled at her blonde friend, then dipped her head, getting ready to take a shot.

My mouth watered when she licked the web between her thumb and pointer finger, getting it ready for her friend to pour salt on. She had a devious-looking smirk on her face, and I counted with her. One. Two. Three.

Next, she sucked the salt off, tossed back the shot, and bit into a lemon. I swallowed hard when a sexy little shiver ran through her. I wanted to be the reason she trembled like that.

"I'll see you back at the house, buddy."

Alex was talking, but I didn't register his words. The brunette dragged her fingers through her hair, pulling it into a high ponytail, revealing a sexy silver layer underneath. This girl was just full of surprises. She fucking owned the hot nerd thing she had going on, and I groaned, tracing the line of her neck. There was a spot below her ear that looked biteable—

A hand landed on my shoulder, snapping me out of my daze, and Alex smirked at me.

"What?" I asked, ignoring the rasp in my throat.

"I said I'd see you at our place." His voice practically screamed, *I told you so.*

The brunette propped her elbows on the table, her back straight and her ass angled out behind her. My pulse kicked up, sending my blood rushing down. Jesus fucking Christ.

"The brunette is mine." I growled the words, and Alex just laughed, smacking my shoulder.

"Yeah, buddy. Tonight's going to be a good fucking time."

As soon as she bent over, all my attention focused on where her fingers glided over the thin band of visible skin between the top of her sock and the bottom of her skirt. I was already walking before she stood. I didn't know who this girl was, but tonight, she was fucking mine.

Alex walked right up to the blonde and gave her a cocky smile. "Besides being sexy, what do you do for a living?"

He should've been arrested for that line, but it hadn't let him down yet. By the way the blonde smiled, it wouldn't fail him now.

The librarian choked on her drink and shook her head. She looked like she was about to say something, but her friend cut in.

"Does that ever work for you?"

Alex moved closer, his voice dropping low. "Don't know. Does it?"

I didn't hear the blonde's reply because now the brunette's attention was on me. Her teeth ran along her bottom lip as her gaze slowly worked its way up my chest. *That's it, baby. Look at me.*

As if she heard my thoughts, her eyes flashed to mine, startling when she found me already watching her. I ran my thumb over my lip, exactly where she gnawed on hers. As a result, her cheeks flushed a deeper pink. So fucking adorable.

"I'm Alex, and this dickhead's Jax. He's been dying to talk to you, so I took pity on him and brought him over."

Fucking asshole. I cut him a glare, but I was distracted when the librarian introduced herself. "Sidney."

Her name felt good rolling over in my head, but before I could say anything, a guy cut between us, wrapping his arm around her waist and handing her a drink. "Drink up. Curtis wants to dance."

He was tall, but not as tall as me, with a lean frame and perfectly styled hair. When she smiled up at him, a jolt ran through me, and a muscle ticked in my jaw. Disappointment mixed with something much more dangerous coursed through me. I tipped back on my heels, needing to get a grip on myself. This girl was fucking trouble.

The guy leaned in closer, his mouth just above her ear, but he spoke loud enough for me to hear. "Oh, he's hot and jealous."

The fuck? He gave her another squeeze, then let go, burying his nose into the neck of the man behind him. In the seconds it took for me to catch up to what was happening, the shorter guy had wrapped his arms around him. Sidney gave them a warm smile, and relief flooded me, knowing the guy was already taken.

He held his hand out. "Hey, man. I'm Anthony, and this is Curtis." He pointed to his boyfriend, who grinned at me.

"Jax." I took a long sip of my beer, and everyone looked at me with identical smiles, but not Sidney. Her gaze was fucking molten. Oh, she liked me jealous. If she stuck around, I had a feeling she'd get what she wanted.

Her friend—I thought she said her name was Mia —grabbed Alex's hand and began tugging him to the dance floor. "Let's dance."

He didn't need any encouragement, already heading in that direction, and Anthony and Curtis followed them.

"We'll catch up in a minute." I stalked toward Sidney, happy she didn't contradict me. No, her gaze was warm on my skin, and there was a slight smile ghosting over her lips. I practically towered over her, her slight frame completely blocked out by my larger one.

The group gave us knowing looks, then dispersed into the crowd.

A giant balloon floating above the table caught my attention. I swear my heart stopped dead as I stared at the blue congratulations balloon with a baby on it. All the blood drained from my head, and my attention went back to Sidney.

I swallowed hard. "Is that for you?"

Her mouth twitched and pulled to the side before she let out a laugh. "You should see your face right now."

Her voice lowered with a subtle rasp, only made sexier by her amusement at the same time her grin grew, until it was practically blinding with pride. "My internship at Parliament was accepted today. Apparently, this was the only congratulations balloon available." She laughed. "Anthony thought it was hilarious."

Not pregnant. My muscles relaxed, and the circulation returned to my body as I slowly registered her words. "No shit, seriously?"

"Don't be too impressed. I need another letter of recommendation. Those two got a little prematurely excited." She nodded, watching me a bit too guarded. I fucking hated that she lost some of her confidence.

I leaned in closer. "Hey, you've got this."

"How can you know that?"

I'm overwhelmed by the need to wipe the unsure look from her face. "I bet you're at the top of your class, right?"

She bit the side of her cheek before answering, "Yeah."

"You've already got other recommendations?"

"Yeah." She stood straighter now. Good.

I pushed harder. "Do you think you can kick your internship's ass?"

She smiled at me, eyes brighter than they were a second ago. "Yeah, I do."

"Then don't worry. You've got this."

She let out a deep breath, and her entire body relaxed. I clipped her chin with my curled forefinger. "I'll leave a good impression on you so you remember me when you make it big."

Heat flushed across her chest, and I followed it up her neck, running my tongue along my top teeth. She was so fucking responsive. I wanted to find out if she blushed like that everywhere. She shifted forward but stopped herself with a hand on the table.

Come on, Sidney. Come get me.

She broke eye contact, looking at her hands. "Do you come here a lot?"

It was a random change of subject, but it was a start. "Enough to know you don't."

She huffed out a laugh and shrugged. "I don't go out much. Busy preparing to be that 'important politician' you were talking about. I've got to keep my image clean."

The things I wanted to do to her were anything but clean. I tipped my voice low until it was a gravelly rumble, forcing her to step into me to hear. "Do you go to school here, Sidney?"

She sucked in a breath when I said her name and bit her lower lip. Fuck. She needed to stop doing that. I was already too fucking turned on.

Her mouth pulled to the side. "Yeah, one semester left. I go to the University of Windsor."

A spark of interest flashed in my chest. "Yeah?"

She gave me a quick nod, and that interest turned to anticipation of seeing more of her.

"Me too. Kinesiology major." I moved in closer

until the toes of our shoes brushed against each other, and she was forced to tip her chin up to meet my gaze. She took a deep breath in, and energy kicked up around us, drawing me closer. I lowered my head above her, keeping my voice steady. "I bet you're a poli-sci, right?"

"You've got it." Her throat lifted with her swallow.

Come on, Trouble. Ask me something.

She didn't disappoint. "So, kinesiology, that's impressive. Planning to work for some pro sports team when you graduate?"

"Something like that." I rolled back on my heels, and she raised a brow. She studied me, clearly not happy with my vague answer, but I didn't want to ruin this moment by bringing that into it.

Sidney stepped back, creating distance between us just as a server walked by. They connected with each other faster than I could warn them, sending Sidney tipping forward. I caught her in my arms, and her touch was like a live wire shooting straight through my veins. The scent of citrus—orange and grapefruit—surrounded me, and I had to fight back a groan. Heat practically poured off her where we connected, soaking into my skin. She stared at my mouth, with heated eyes. She didn't move, and I didn't interrupt her as she took me in fully. Fuck, the way she was staring at me turned me the fuck on. I swallowed hard, then lowered my lips above her ear and murmured, "Caught you."

"I... I didn't mean—" she said, flustered.

Deciding to put her out of her misery, I gestured toward our friends. "At this point, if Alex gets any closer to Mia, they're going to become one."

She lifted onto her toes, placing a hand on my shoulder for balance, and craned her neck to see them. I knew she felt my low rumble under her soft touch.

Her fingers curled into my shirt, but she didn't face me when she said, "Is he always like this?"

I lowered my chin to her ear, focused on the millions of goosebumps that rose over her skin. "A shameless flirt? Pretty much."

Sidney leaned back, her gaze traveling from my mouth to my eyes, and I spread my fingers over her back, tugging her closer. She made a soft sound that had my breath catching in my throat and my dick growing hard. I searched her face, wanting—no, *needing*—to know that she felt this too. That I wasn't the only one driven fucking crazy just being near her.

A sensual grin formed on her mouth. "Are you hitting on me?"

"Maybe. Is it working?"

Her smile grew. "Maybe."

My grip tightened, her words sounding distinctly like a yes. She was throwing off *fuck me* signals, and god, I hoped I was right. I paused, not sure where to go from here. At first, I found her hot, but fuck if I wasn't more interested now. There was something about her. She was clearly smart, and there was a level of sass coming off of her that had me itching to—

"Want to dance?" Sidney asked, cutting off my thoughts.

"Fuck yes." I practically growled the words, and I was rewarded by her shiver. Sidney entwined our fingers, and I followed her like a lost puppy, but who could fucking blame me? She looked delicious in her short plaid skirt with a white slim-fitting T-shirt that had come loose.

Sidney picked a spot on the dance floor out of sight of our friends, turned to face away from me, and swayed to the beat. She moved in slow, languid motions that made my dick harder with each second I watched her. My hands curled with restraint, and Sidney's breath caught in her throat when they landed on her hips, tugging her back into my chest. *Fuck.* She rolled against me until her ass pushed into my groin, driving me insane. My mind chanted the same thing over and over, like some kind of fucking caveman. *Mine.*

I needed to take her home tonight, or it would fucking kill me.

Blood rushed to my already rock-hard cock when I ran my fingers just below her skirt and squeezed her exposed thighs. A low growl escaped the back of my throat when her entire body trembled in my grasp. Fuck, she didn't know how close she had me to the edge. She leaned her head on my shoulder, tilting it to the side, making room for my mouth, and hummed when I licked up the narrow column of her neck.

"You smell so fucking good." I groaned, burying my face in her shoulder.

She whimpered, and I flipped her to face me, needing to capture it with my mouth. We were so close her breath fanned over my lips, but she tucked her chin to stop the kiss.

The fuck? I dropped my forehead to hers, breathing in each of her breaths. Sidney's hands ran up my abdomen, and I groaned deeply when she dug her nails into my chest. Her lips were pink where she bit into them, and I fucking craved to run my tongue along the marks. Her mouth formed a perfect pout, and I shifted close enough that it nearly brushed mine with each inhale.

Sidney made a low, pained sound before jerking her head back. She sucked in several breaths, and her eyes widened on me.

Ice filled my veins, replacing the heat that had been building. Did I read her wrong? Did I push her too far? "I'm sorry. Whatever I did, I'm fucking sorry."

She let out a long sigh, then shook her head, a smirk forming on her full lips. "That's rule number one: no kissing."

She shifted back a few inches, and my hands tightened on her hips, not letting her go. My gaze flicked from her mouth to her eyes and back, trying to process anything but the desire to taste her. I dragged my teeth over my bottom lip, and she tracked the movement while her tongue wet hers. Sidney's words finally broke through the haze of lust, and they hit harder than they should. "What?"

"Rule number one." She leaned away, but her fingers still dug into me like she didn't want to let me go. Good. I didn't fucking want her to.

My gaze searched hers as if I would find the answer there. Sidney was already turning away, but I caught the disappointed look in her eyes. She gestured to her table with her thumb. "I need a drink."

Me fucking too, Sidney.

She pulled from my grasp, and I immediately missed the feel of her. What the hell was happening? One minute, we were all over each other, and the next, I stood here stunned. She was already at the table before I snapped out of it.

"What do you mean rule?" I asked as soon as I reached her.

She finished her tall glass in a few sips. "Just what I said. I have rules for this type of thing."

"What sort of thing?"

"One-night stands."

"What if I want it to be longer?" Where the fuck did that come from?

"That's rule number two: one night only."

My brows pinched together, not sure what to make of it. I should've been happy she was down for one night. Hell, I should've been ecstatic. What guy didn't want that? Apparently me, because her taking more off the table didn't sit right.

Curious, I played along. "Okay, I can respect your game."

Her glare was ruined when she hiccupped. "Rules, not a game."

My hands rose in surrender. "Sorry. Rules."

"That's better. Look, we're getting way off course here. You're hot. I'm pretty sure you think I'm hot. Come home with me." She hiccupped between her words and swayed on her feet.

I caught her, holding her closer than necessary, and tried not to preen when she wrapped her hands around my back. Her pupils were blown wide, and I swallowed hard when her tongue snuck out, wetting her bottom lip.

So fucking pissed at what was about to come out of my mouth, but I'd never been and would never be the type of guy who brought a drunk girl home. No matter how tempting she was. "It fucking kills me to say this. And it *really* fucking does, but you've had too much to drink tonight for this conversation."

She frowned.

I slid my phone toward her. "How about you give me your number and we can do this again? Sober."

She chuckled, shaking her head. "Nope, can't do that."

I raked my fingers through my hair. "Tell me this isn't another rule."

Sidney propped her chin on my chest and smirked, looking sexy as fuck. I tipped my head back to the ceiling and took in a deep breath. Please, fucking god. This couldn't be happening. I had never chased a girl in my fucking life, and this girl had me hooked. "What if I gave you mine?"

She scrunched her nose. Fucking adorable. "Rule number three: no exchanging phone numbers."

"How the fuck does that work?" I had to stop myself from tightening my grip. I was getting dangerously close to being an asshole, but come the fuck on. These rules were killing me. "What happens if you're into a guy?" If only my boys could see me now. I'd never live it down.

She gave me an apologetic smile, and I already knew what was coming. "Breaks rule number five."

"Tell me," I deadpanned.

"Being into a guy leads to dating, dating leads to relationships, and relationships lead to feelings. Rule number five: no falling in love."

A muscle ticked in my jaw. "How many rules do you have?"

"Five."

"What's the fourth rule?" Someone grabbed my shoulder, twisting me to face him and effectively cutting me off.

"Congrats, buddy. That goal was insane," he screamed over the music, and his breath reeked of beer.

"Goal?" Sidney's head tilted to the side, looking me up and down as if seeing me for the first time.

The big guy beside me wore my team's teal hockey jersey. He turned around, showing her the back, where the last name Ryder was written across it in large white letters. He faced her and smiled.

"Yeah, sweetheart. You going to pretend you don't know you're hooking up with the Huskies' star forward?"

"Jax Ryder?" she asked with a little shake of her head like she was telling me to say no.

"Yeah." I swallowed hard. For the first time, I got the impression my name was going to backfire on me.

Her shoulders slumped, and she looked so fucking disappointed before lifting onto her toes and leaning closer to me. Her eyes were wide as she searched my face, and I wished I could make out their color in the dim club light. I reveled in the heat of her body pressed tightly against my chest as she brought her mouth closer to mine, so close I could feel her breath fan across mine. My mouth watered, and it took everything in me not to close the distance. *Come on, Trouble. Kiss me.*

"That's really too bad, Jax." She closed the distance, kissing me just to the side of my lips, then broke away from my arms, brows pulled together. She took a step toward her friends, nearly tripping as she did. I so wanted to help her, but her words caught me up. "Rule number four: no hockey players."

"You've got to be kidding me."

"Nope." She gave me a downcast smirk and wiggled her fingers goodbye before turning around.

My gaze tracked her ass the entire time, and a slow smile curved across my lips. I never could resist breaking the rules.

Keep reading for the steamy, kick your feet in the air inducing, heartfelt, college hockey romance, Rule Number Five.

Available on Amazon at https://amzn.to/40pYmvt

STALK ME!

Follow Jessa on:
Tik Tok:
Jesswilderauthor

Instagram:
Jessicawilderauthor

Website:
jessawilder.com

ACKNOWLEDGMENTS

Thank you to my three super star Alpha readers. You are amazing.
Thank you for putting up with me when I bug you all day.
Thank you for cheering me on even when I have crazy ideas like randomly writing a novella.

Thank you to the readers who came in clutch last minute to help me catch those pesky typos!

Love you.

ALSO BY

Rule Number Five
Book 1 in the Rule Breaker Series
<u>READ NOW</u>
I had my whole life planned out... until I met a hockey player obsessed with breaking all of my rules.

My 5 simple rules for hooking up keep me from being distracted. And now I'm so close to landing my dream internship. Nothing is going to make me break them.

Even a protective hockey player with clear grey eyes, a sharp jaw, and a body that makes my breath catch.

Until Jax wins a bet and one kiss has me breaking them all.

TROPES:
· Slowburn
· He Falls First
· Friends with benefits

· Jealousy

· Mutual pining

Rules Of The Game

Book 2 in the Rule Breaker Series

READ NOW

He's the star hockey player, my brother's best friend and the boy I've been in love with since I was 7.

The problem? He wants nothing to do with me.

Then why does he sneak into my room when I have a nightmare?

Gets jealous when I go on a date?

And has a tattoo of my birthday on his ribs.

Lucas Knight's a lot of things. He's possessive, jealous and overprotective. And he just might be in love with me.

Angst filled, heartbreaking and kick your feet in the air giddy inducing.

TROPES:

* *Brother's Best Friend*

* *Secret Pen Pal*

* *Jealousy*

* *Mutual pining*

* *You're going to suffer, but you're going to be happy about it.*

The Gentlemen Series

READ NOW

She's a kickass thief and the heads of her rival gang, Beck, Nico, and Rush need her help.

Whychoose, Multi-POV, Badass Heroine, Tons of funny banter, All over 20 years old, Forced Proximity
By Jessa Wilder & Kate King
The Blissful Omegaverse Series
<u>**READ NOW**</u>
In a world where Omegas are cherished, Alphas are revered, and Betas are forgotten I wouldn't have changed a thing.

Growing up in foster care, my friends and I took care of each other. Ares, Killian, Rafe, and Nox, were my everything: my first loves, my only family, my pack. Until the same night they told me we'd be together forever, I presented as an Omega, and everything changed. By Jessa Wilder & Kate King

Made in United States
North Haven, CT
11 July 2024

54583777R00075